PRAISE FOR CORM

FAITH MERINO

CORMORANT LAKE

A NOVEL

**BLACK
STONE**
PUBLISHING

Printed in the United States of America
Originally published in hardcover by Blackstone Publishing in 2021

First paperback edition: 2022
ISBN 979-8-200-83417-4
Fiction / Literary

Version 1

CIP data for this book is available
from the Library of Congress

Blackstone Publishing
31 Mistletoe Rd.
Ashland, OR 97520

www.BlackstonePublishing.com

For Travis, Jack, and Edwin

THE LEAVING

It was because of the bathtub that she left with the two little girls in the night, dresser drawers pulled out and moved whole into the car, T-shirts and jackets stuffed into trash bags with Barbie dolls and blankies and binkies, everything hefted out to her idling sangria-red '92 Toyota Corolla. She'd already stocked the back seat with raisins, graham crackers, and two boxes of Lucky Charms because they were Lila's favorite—and the toddler had a big and constant hunger, even though she was all tender bones.

Evelyn was good at moving silently, and she had to get the girls out of the house without waking anyone, because she'd drawn a line at finding the baby in the bathtub, twisting like an alligator underwater.

First she got Lila, whose lean little goat legs dangled as Evelyn carried her through the house that smelled like ashes, lighter fluid, and sulfur—a cutting chemical sharpness. Underneath: a fungal human smell. Yeasty.

She laid Lila down in the back seat, folding the three-year-old's legs and tucking the blanket around them before she went back for Mora. She lifted the baby—a little over a year old,

1

FAITH MERINO

maybe more—out of the torn playpen, carefully wrapping her in blankets to keep her asleep on the way out. Her hair was still wet and Evelyn smelled it deeply as she laid her down next to Lila. Mora's eyes only briefly fluttered before she rolled onto her side, pressed her face into the back of the seat, and shuddered out a long sigh.

Evelyn got in the car and drove away from the house.

She drove slowly, cautiously, using her turn signals, keeping below the speed limit as she merged onto the 91. She planned to be out of California by the time the girls' mother woke up.

EVELYN

A November sun came up over the eastern mountains as Evelyn drove north on the 5 through California's central valley—thousands of acres of almond orchards and orange groves spinning off into the foothills, morning fog creeping out from the mountains. Her defroster was broken and she had to turn on the fan to clear the clouding windows. When her eyes got heavy and sleep came creeping in like water rising in a basement, she rolled her window down and let cold air blast her face until her eyes leaked, just like Doris Clearwater's leaky eyes—always damp for some reason.

Doris Clearwater, drying her eyes with her sleeve as she said, "This is Erin. She's going to crash for a while." And there was Erin: wide forehead, eyes too big for her face, slender nose almost disappearing between her broad cheekbones. A toddler holding her hand, and in the crook of one elbow, the tiniest pink baby Evelyn had ever seen. Lila and Mora.

The girls woke sometime after sunrise with yawns and slow blinks. Lila sat up and her eyelashes blazed gold as they drove through an almond orchard, sun flashing between the trees.

"I got to potty," she said.

Evelyn pulled the car onto the side of the road and got Lila out, put her little pink flip-flops on her feet before setting her on the ground. She held the skinny girl by the armpits so she could squat and pee in the dirt, chips of brown glass glittering around them. The wind whipped their hair, and the T-shirt Lila wore as a nightgown snapped as Evelyn tried to hold it out of the pee stream. By the time Lila was done, she was shivering, legs shaking as she balanced on her toes. Evelyn lifted her back into the car and got back on the freeway.

She was slow and careful, so the trip took a full day. They passed reeking dairy farms where manure had been bulldozed into tarped mountains, the plastic weighted down with old tires. The chemical stink followed them for miles, even when they'd gotten upwind of it.

It had been years since she'd driven this stretch of the 5 and everything looked the same. It felt like she'd been in this exact moment before, even though she hadn't gone home since she left.

They drove past rice paddies and strawberry fields, through sulfurous clouds of garlic and cabbage, and the briny smell of the sea as they passed the San Joaquin River, where the salmon were spawning and dying on the riverbanks.

She tucked towels in the windows so no one would see two children rolling around in the back. When the girls got antsy and climbed over the seats to pull her hair, she steered with her knees and poked straws into juice boxes for them. Mora squeezed too hard and dribbled red all over her sleep shirt. Evelyn opened the second box of Lucky Charms for their lunch.

At a rest stop, she changed the baby's diaper in the trunk. Afterward, she dressed them both in leggings and sweaters and set them on the wet grass to stomp around while she filled a thermos and two baby bottles with water from the drinking fountain. Before they left, she took Lila to the bathroom, lifting her onto the toilet by one arm as she held the baby on her hip to keep her off the grimy, wet floor, but she couldn't catch Lila before she slipped and grabbed the foul toilet seat with both hands.

On the freeway again, she checked her rearview mirror. With each mile she put between them and the house in Riverside, with its dirt yard and cracked siding, she could exhale more deeply, letting her ribs settle.

Slowly, the valley flatland and bald, brown foothills gave way to twisted oaks that hunched on their knuckles. The oaks heaved into ponderosa pines, and then, as they crossed into Washington, to towering red cedars, mountains bristling with Sitka spruces and Douglas firs.

It was evening when the trees cleared to reveal the wide, snaking S of Cormorant Lake, shaped like a bird's neck and gleaming gray under heavy thunderheads. The mountains rose blue and cold out of the water like Titans, furred with ancient pines and dusted with recent snowfall. Somewhere below them, two thousand feet beneath the lake's surface, a derailed train lay hidden in the black sediment depths.

Evelyn hugged bends in the wet road that disappeared between the towering walls of hemlocks, cedars, and dripping maples. To her right, a formation of Canada geese cut down the mountainside and sailed across the lake, gliding into the water in a skidding spray. Likely the first geese of the season. They usually came to roost in the darkest months of winter—December and January—before moving on.

She turned onto a mud-and-gravel road, car jouncing in the deep ruts as the road coiled higher into the hills past squatty, square houses with boarded-up windows and rotting porches, yards scattered with rusting trucks and lawn mowers, faded and busted up kids' toys, soda cans, beer bottles, and tarps pooled with brown water. Drive strips made of wooden planks were set over slough ditches. A skinny man, hunched over and rangy as a rosebush, drank from a thermos at a camper shell he was using as a table.

A memory: Packy drinking from a thermos in his pickup truck in the red flush of a California sunrise, face striped blue from the tinted strip of the windshield.

And there at the top of the hill, hidden in a sanctum of firs and maples, was the little house she'd left fourteen years ago—a simple white bungalow, mud-spattered latticework covering the porch, roof grown thick and iridescent green with moss.

She parked in the packed-mud-and-gravel driveway. Lila and Mora had both fallen asleep in the back seat, and Evelyn lifted them out and carried them up the porch steps. The kitchen light was on and she could see Nan at the sink, could see the broad slope of her back as she washed the dishes from the dinner she'd made for herself. Always a firm believer in the importance of good posture, Nan stood with her shoulders high and back tight—"Imagine pinching a safety pin between your shoulder blades."

She must have heard Evelyn's boots on the porch because she looked up, frowning, and moved toward the door—the sore-kneed stomping as she crossed the floor, the low, muscular trot of Rosie, the pit mix, close behind, and when Nan opened the door, she was old. Her seventy-ninth birthday had passed that September and there were starbursts of lines at the corners of her eyes, which instantly flashed wet with tears—then she was reaching out with both hands and pulling Evelyn's head to hers. She was crying.

Nan pulled away and looked at Mora and Lila. "You have

babies," she said. "But you didn't tell me. You never told me." She went on blinking for another moment, then wiped her eyes with trembling hands. "Come on."

They went inside the house, which was exactly as Evelyn remembered it—the couch and love seat in an L that took up the whole room, piano by the window, doilies on the end tables, and books stacked in a cubby under the coffee table. Evelyn breathed the clean smell of fresh laundry, the sharp undercurrent of ammonia, but also the staleness of settled dust, like the windows hadn't been opened in years.

"You know, a storm just came through and there was a landslide in Ozette. Did you hear about this?" said Nan, as if picking up a conversation they'd been having. "It unearthed human remains. Carbon dating determined they were from eight thousand years ago! Likely people who'd migrated from the Bering Land Bridge. Scientists think they were buried when the mountain exploded. It was all over the news."

Lila and Mora ran through the house, small feet thumping loudly across the floor as they chased one another up and down the hall. Rosie hid under the table, heavy head on her paws as her eyes followed them. Each of her eyebrows lifted alternately with concern. Just a puppy when Evelyn left, now she was gray-faced.

In any other house, Evelyn would call to the girls, tell them to stop running, but they were restless from the drive and she knew that Nan would forgive. They found the piano and slammed their palms on the keys discordantly. Lila stopped, grabbed her crotch with a squat, and then ran into the bathroom. In another moment she was singing, which was what she always did when she was pooping, and when she yelled, "Mama!" Evelyn went to the bathroom to wipe her.

Nan made a pot of coffee. On the counter was a homemade

frosted sheet cake covered in plastic wrap. There were two empty squares. Nan didn't ask before she took the plastic wrap off and got four small plates out of the cupboard. She paused.

"The baby probably won't eat a whole piece on her own. You think they'll share?"

Evelyn waved her hand. "They don't need no cake—any cake. They've had plenty of sugar. And besides, it's almost their bedtime."

Nan ignored her and cut three pieces, slicing the third in half and splitting it between two plates. She brought the cake to the table and went back to the kitchen to get forks, napkins, and mugs for the coffee.

As Nan stomped quickly through the kitchen, Evelyn scanned the walls. Same pictures and devotional cards, shelves cluttered with decorative plates: shimmering, metallic images of the Virgin Mary and Jesus with sunbeams bursting from his flaming heart. Everywhere, there were portraits and statuettes of the Blessed Virgin and different saints. Nan's favorites were Saint Elizabeth Ann Seton, who taught girls in the late eighteenth century, and Saint Cecilia, who was struck three times by the sword during her unsuccessful beheading but lived for three more days. Nan liked stories about defiant women.

Evelyn spotted the black-and-white newspaper clipping of the deformed toddler. It was still on Nan's wall, right above her foldout writing desk—Peter Lark, the Boy Without a Face. A toddler sitting on a table stared from eyeless sockets—tunnels of black collapsing on themselves. His mouth was a black gash curving up on the left side of his face, his nose a taut nub of skin with two asymmetrical nostrils. His airy blond hair was tufted and sticking up on one side, as if he'd woken from a nap. A lean, dark-haired man stood over him, hands on the table, arms locked on either side of the boy as he stared out of the picture with pale, cut glass eyes. Doctor Linden.

Nan brought out her mother's sugar bowl with the glazed-over crack in the rim and the matching creamer pitcher, which she filled before bringing it to the table. She poured the coffee into a carafe and sat down at the table with Evelyn, long enough for Evelyn to take a breath and say, "They ain't mine."

Nan looked at her, hands moving of their own accord as she took up the carafe and poured coffee into Evelyn's mug.

"Aren't mine," Evelyn corrected herself.

"Whose are they?" Nan asked.

"A friend's."

Nan didn't stir her coffee. She always poured the cream in her mug first and then poured in the coffee so it mixed at once. No sugar. Evelyn had always wondered if it was just because Nan didn't want one more spoon to wash.

"Why do you have them?" Nan asked, sipping her coffee.

And Evelyn told her—some things, not others. She told her about Erin, who was a cigarette burn in a film reel, never really there; never really gone. She came and went. No one ever knew for sure if she was home when they heard the baby crying in the next room, until eventually someone would open her bedroom door and find the two little girls alone in the room—no Erin.

She told Nan about the morning one year ago, when she came home to an empty house after being gone for a week with Packy, and found the girls in the playpen—no food, lips flaking with dehydration, a single rank, empty bottle left behind. She fed them, gave them water, cleaned them up because they'd been in the same diapers for days. Evelyn didn't know exactly when Erin had left, but she'd left for good.

Evelyn told Nan about buying diapers and baby formula.

How she got two car seats from a yard sale. Got the old woman next door to babysit while she went to work. Took the girls to parks on her days off. Bought baby clothes and a high chair from a thrift store. The girls both started calling her Mama—Mora's first word. They slept in her bed, their hot hands on her face and neck as they snored.

Evelyn had been their mother for nearly a year when Erin came through the front door one night, clear-eyed, fresh as milk, saying, "Where're my babies at?" She'd gotten clean. She moved the girls back into her room.

Nan listened and sipped her coffee, never betraying any alarm or shock, not even when Evelyn told her about coming home last night and finding the baby twisting in the bathtub—about putting the girls in the car and leaving because she had to get them far away from Erin.

"Will their mother look for them?" Nan finally asked.

"I think so. Probably."

Nan nodded, but didn't say anything as she reached across the table to cut up a too-big chunk of cake that Lila was trying to muscle off her plate. Lila stared at Nan with large eyes, and quickly forked a piece into her mouth. In another moment, the rest of the slice was gone.

"I just want my girls to grow up right," Evelyn said.

Nan looked at her, a sharp edge in her stare, like she'd heard something familiar.

Evelyn said, "They're mine."

Mora was lumbering up and down the hallway, taking wide, spraddle-legged baby steps and babbling. Her slice sat on its own plate at an empty chair and Evelyn wondered if she should call Mora over to eat, to be polite to Nan. She pulled the plate over to Lila instead.

"Here. Have Mora's," she said. "This is really good. Thank

you," she said to Nan, because Nan had taught her that it was important to always thank the host.

Lila stabbed into Mora's cake, panting out little puffs of breath between bites so she could eat more quickly. Nan watched her, and then put her hands on the table, leaned in, and said to Lila, "I have ice cream. Do you want ice cream?"

Lila's mouth was open and she nodded as the tip of her tongue licked frosting off the corner of her mouth.

The next morning, Evelyn dug a perimeter trench two feet wide, two feet deep—a border around the house. A protective spell.

Her breath fogged in the dense, cold air as she pushed the shovel into the earth and the blade cut through the black mud. Sunless, the sky was a jaundiced gray. The whole mountain would have been a dull bleed of color if it weren't for the blazing gold leaves of the aspens that bordered the southern edge of the property. But soon, Evelyn knew, the leaves would fall, and the stand of aspens would look like a jagged boneyard in the mist.

She hadn't planned to dig the trench. She'd started inside the house, tearing out the rotting walls and floorboards in her old room to show Nan she was truly staying. Black mold was creeping up the wall like a poxy blue-black rash in the corner, freckling its way into the living room, the guest-room closet, behind the kitchen table.

The house had always been waterlogged, and as she ripped open the soft walls, they exhaled a damp, cavernous smell, like sitting water and rock. Deep. In the summer, her bedroom would take on a mildew smell like the swampy underbelly of a wet dog.

While carrying the torn drywall out, she'd noticed that the

front door was swollen shut. To go outside, she had to grab the knob with both hands and throw herself backward to yank it open, and then slam a shoulder against it to shut it again.

The problem wasn't actually the door, but the rain gutter, which was clogged with leaves and eaten through with rust. The leak over the front door caused water to splatter against door and frame, making them both swell. The rain gutter would need to be replaced. There was another leak over the corner of the porch, which had left the wood warped and slick with a film of bottle-fly-green slime.

Evelyn threw the drywall pieces on the lawn and got the ladder out of the garage. She climbed up and unscrewed the gutters one section at a time, then carried them back to the garage, placing them on the workbench so the girls wouldn't cut themselves on the sharp metal. As she was leaving, she saw the constellation of furry black mold in the corner near the back door. The problem, then, was deeper. Something from the outside getting in.

Evelyn walked to the end of the driveway and looked at the house and the ground around it. If the house were a painting, the lines would all be sinking in at the center. The house was at a slightly lower grade than the land around it, which meant groundwater was pooling under the foundation.

She rubbed her eyes, itchy with lost sleep, and went back inside where Nan was sitting at the table with Lila and Mora, watching them eat bowls of ice cream. Mora was sitting on two phone books, pink feet twirling, looking at Evelyn with her big, soft owl eyes. Erin's eyes. With her high forehead and small, pointed chin, they had almost the exact same face.

"They can't eat ice cream for breakfast," said Evelyn.

"Why can't they? They like it."

"Well—yeah, they like it. It's ice cream."

Lila threw her hands in the air, fingers splayed. "Ice cream!"

"What's the difference between this and that sugary cereal and red drink you give them?" Nan asked.

Evelyn was too tired to argue. She couldn't say why cereal and juice boxes were better for the girls than ice cream.

Nan leaned over the table to look into Lila's empty bowl. "My goodness. Someone was hungry. How about seconds?"

She stood up and Lila followed her to the freezer.

"Nan," Evelyn sighed.

Nan ignored her as she got the carton of mint chip out of the freezer and began scooping another bowl for Lila, who bobbled on the balls of her feet, making a strange, throaty growl sound. She ran to the table, stabbing her spoon into the bowl before Nan had even set it down.

"I gotta go to the hardware store to get some things. Back in a few," Evelyn said as she grabbed her keys and wallet.

The hum of the engine was lulling and Evelyn had to focus as she drove down the rutted mud-and-gravel road until it turned into asphalt. She made a left onto Main Street, everything damp from a night rain, and drove past Cormorant Lake High School, a stern two-story structure that was built in the 1910s, the redbrick facade blackened with mold, as if scorched by fire. Teenagers were huddling together on the front lawn. A throng of teenage boys had gathered in front of the school sign and one of them—a boy in baggy black jeans—shoved another into the street, forcing Evelyn to brake hard. The boy in the street laughed at Evelyn and slapped the hood of her car hard before walking lazily back to the others. Evelyn's ears roared with blood as she drove slowly away. She'd gone to Cormorant Lake High with boys like that.

She drove past the Native Touch massage spa, which took up the bottom floor of the Victorian building that had once been the Stadler Hotel. A woman in tight jeans was leaning against the window, texting underneath a giant, painted pair of brown hands braceleted in abalone shells. The man in the car ahead of Evelyn called out to the woman, who looked up from her phone and yelled, "Fuck you!"

Evelyn opened her eyes wide, squeezed them shut tight, and strained to focus on the road, fighting off the slow drip of sleep because she'd lain awake the previous night. She hadn't slept in forty-eight hours.

She drove past the Tooley Lumberyard, with its smells of hot sawdust and stacks of heartwood so fresh it steamed in the cold. Past the nearby Tooley Hotel, built around the same time as the Stadler Hotel by the Tooley Timber Company, and which was now a restaurant and vacant offices.

If she kept driving north, she'd find herself on the Makah Reservation, from which her father had come, according to her mother. Evelyn had never seen it, had no memory of her father. Her mother had only told her about his hair—long, curly, because he got it permed.

Evelyn turned into the Linden Hardware parking lot, parked, and stepped out into the bracing lake wind that smelled like deep water, black pine mud, and leaking motor oil. Inside, the store was warm and the white linoleum floor had been waxed to a blazing, blinding brilliance. Squinting against the light, she bought four coils of drainage pipe, some filter paper, and six bags of gravel. She didn't have the money for galvanized steel or aluminum, so she bought one hundred twenty feet of vinyl gutters, some elbows and brackets, some downspouts and corner joints, and some end caps and strip miters. Altogether, the materials cost three hundred forty-six dollars, which was the last of her money.

She piled the gravel and gutters in the trunk of her Corolla, and heaped the rest in the back seat.

As she drove away, she thought the cashier had looked familiar—the way her face rounded into the timorous dip of the chin, the eyes that cut upward in the outer corners. But it was a feeling not of having known her before, but of having encountered her in this exact moment at this exact hardware store already.

Packy believed déjà vu happened when someone encountered a moment in time they had already visited somewhere else in the multiverse.

"If the odds of the universe being just the right size to support life are millions to one," he'd told her, "then what if that means there are millions—billions, trillions—of other universes out there, universes that flung themselves too far for life to take hold—and millions, billions, and trillions of other universes that have succeeded?" Smiling, hands flapping the way they did when he got excited and didn't have a cigarette to hold, his eyes on hers—eyes bright with a solar radiance, wanting to see everything. "What if a new universe is born every second, every half second—as easily as a cell divides—and they're all layered on top of each other like a deck of cards? Occupying the same space, just on different frequencies? And what if in those other universes, we're born, we grow, and we choose differently? What if we're passing ourselves every day?"

The next day, Packy was gone—had disappeared in the night without even waking Evelyn to tell her goodbye, but he did that so often that it would be another two weeks before she'd realize he wasn't coming back.

She wasn't metaphysical enough. Too heavy, too earthbound to skate with him along the outer edges of the swirling galactic arms.

Now, as she dug and turned the black earth, slowly bringing the ends of the circle together, she realized that Lila was following her. She'd come out, with her frizzy Barbie dolls, to sit down in the grass and quietly make the dolls talk to each other.

"You want some cake? Yes, I love some. You want ice cream? Yes, I love ice cream."

Soft, slightly muffled piano music came from inside the house as Nan played by the window, the notes haphazard at first but then braiding together in an orderly rhythm that Evelyn, Lila, and Rosie all moved to. Chopin. One of Nan's favorites.

Rosie followed Lila at a distance, curious but wary. She lay down in the grass a few yards away to watch Lila play, tail wagging in contained eagerness.

"You want some bananas? No, not like bananas," Lila said, waving one doll at the other.

Evelyn laughed and Lila looked at her with a grim, demanding stare. Lila hated bananas. She would eat them, but the texture made her gag, made her eyes water.

Lila had a bottomless hunger and would eat anything, even if she hated it—Evelyn had learned that back in Riverside. It had been there, in the windy, sand-scraped desert, while replacing cracked siding on the house for Doris Clearwater, that Evelyn saw Lila in the backyard eating honeysuckle flowers off the fence. Erin had just moved in and twice put Lila outside in the yard and locked the door. In the midday heat, the pale toddler—skin like thin blue milk, with crackling electric veins in her temples—had crammed fistfuls of honeysuckle flowers in her mouth, then crawled under the back porch to sleep in the shade. Evelyn knew that going after the little girl meant never getting out of it, but she set the siding down and crouched down to peer under the porch—found Lila curled on her side in the dirt—and picked her up.

She carried Lila around the house and through the unlocked front door, into the sulfurous living room with its musty shag carpet and the warped wall-furnace grill, past the bathroom door that didn't shut all the way because someone had once kicked it in. She set Lila down at the kitchen table and made her a peanut butter sandwich, then another, and poured a glass of water that Lila spilled down her front. When Lila caught her breath, she grabbed a torn envelope from a pile of junk mail on the table and handed it to Evelyn, saying, "You draw a dog for me?" So Evelyn did, doodling a cartoonish picture of a dog and handing the envelope back to Lila, who held it at arm's length to inspect it and smiled.

Erin would know by now. They'd been gone two days. Had she called the cops? Would she call the cops?

Of course she would. She was a mother.

Evelyn pushed her shovel into the earth and dug the circle closed.

NAN

Nan's car bounced and rollicked along the rutted road, and Rosie sat upright in the passenger's seat, unfazed, as Nan drove down the hill into town. They passed the yellow blinking traffic light that swayed on a wire over the four-way stop at Main and Evergreen, and continued into the woods on the other side. Normally she walked it, but today there wasn't time, and she parked on the side of the road, got out with her gardening tools in hand. Rosie followed her through the dripping trees, head low as she sniffed and rooted and ate the forest floor. But Rosie knew where Nan was headed so she cut ahead toward the old church.

Nan walked behind her, and eventually they came to the clearing where the old wall stood—the last remnant of the original Catholic church that had once sat on a low hillside overlooking the dock. The landslide of 1962 had taken everything—the original lumberyard, the rail station, the Methodist church, the graveyards. It had taken the Catholic church, but left this one section of wall—an alcove where the statue of the Virgin Mary still stood, half hidden in a thicket of huge ferns that were reaching out of the mortar. The statue used to be white, but a constant stream of water pouring from a remaining lip of wall above had stained it green.

Nan kissed her fingers and pressed them to the Virgin's toes as Rosie trotted ahead to sniff the animal wildness in the scrub. Trees grew fast, and all the trees in this part of the woods had risen from the newly piled earth in the years following the landslide, as if nothing else had ever been here.

The church had been around when Nan was a girl growing up in Cormorant Lake. She'd gotten married in this church, a ceremony that her mother and father had refused to attend because Earl was a timberman with no future after a logging-camp fire melted his right hand into a fist, months before their wedding.

She'd grown up in a little house just up the western path, with a wrought iron gate and rosebushes hemming the yard that she wasn't allowed to leave. In the small sitting room, there had been a piano that her mother had brought with them from the north shore of the lake, back when her parents had money, before her father's bad investments sent their wealth arcing out on a whip that never cracked back in. They had kept just enough to afford a housekeeper—Clara's mother. But Nan wasn't allowed to play with the south shore children, not even Clara, so she played the piano. The house had been too small for such a big sound, but her parents never made her stop.

The house was gone now, taken by the mountain.

Nan unwound the rosary from the Virgin's praying hands and dried the beads on her sweater to clean off the algae before winding them back around the cold plaster hands. Then she closed her eyes, pressed her hands over her face, and prayed—prayed that the McNealy sisters would have simultaneous heart attacks, wander into traffic, or get snatched by mountain lions. Maybe one could choke on a sandwich and the other could die of grief. Or they could both slip comfortably into senility and forget they ever saw Evelyn and the strange, red-haired girl who looked nothing like her.

They'd come by that morning, walking their little dogs up the hill, and when Nan saw the skinny, stoop-shouldered old sisters walking past her house and stopping to smile at Evelyn on the ladder, she said out loud, "I hate those bitches."

"Evie? Is that my Evie?" Myrna had called as her wispy Pomeranian twitched on its leash.

Evelyn was screwing the new rain gutters onto the house. Myrna was smiling, showing her teeth, while Helen looked down at the ground, chin tucked, her throat always contracted like she was gagging quietly to herself—and not ten feet away from them, Lila sat in the wet lawn, feeding plastic toy food to an imaginary friend.

Nan watched from the window as Lila stared, red curls floating in the pine wind, green globe eyes clicking into focus. Lila and Mora were river sprites, fish-boned fairy children—they looked nothing like Evelyn with her cavernous black eyes and ice-cliff cheekbones. They were water to her earth.

"Hi, Granny. Hi, MeeMaw," Evelyn said, because that's what Myrna and Helen made everyone call them. The two sisters gave powerful hugs, remembered birthdays, and had been telling children to call them Granny and MeeMaw since they were in their forties. But they were mean. They would come over to Nan's house with bowls of mealy strawberries from their gardens to gossip about everyone. About Dulcey who used to be such a cute thing and now she didn't wash her hair and never cleaned her trailer. About Harvey who got Katrina Meurer pregnant and gave her money for an abortion. About that sweet tomboy Cally who now had terrible psoriasis and was rumored to be dating a black boy.

The last thing Nan needed was those mean old bitches telling the town about Evelyn's new daughters.

"Evie, come down here and give me a hug. I ain't seen you in ages," called Myrna.

Nan cleared her throat and went outside to get Lila.

"Come on, sweet pea. Let's go inside. Myrna! Helen! How are you?" she asked, hauling Lila up by the armpits and steering her back into the house.

"Evie, is that your little girl?" asked Myrna, pointing at Lila, who was walking slowly into the house, the seat of her jeans soaked through from the grass.

Nan shut the door after Lila.

"She's beautiful. She looks just like you," Myrna said with practiced warmth.

"Thanks," Evelyn said with a nervous waver that traveled on a frequency only Nan could hear.

"I think she looks more like her father—another man with a wandering eye. Useless cheat," said Nan, hands on hips.

"Well come down here and tell us all about her! I want to know where you've been the last—has it been fifteen years?"

"I gotta get these gutters done, but I promise I'll come by soon and tell you all about it, Granny," said Evelyn, who stared down at the McNealy sisters with her shoulders hunched up—the way she used to look at adults when she was little: refusing to speak, eyes glassy bright. Distrustful.

Now, Nan kissed her fingers and pressed them to the Virgin's feet one more time, lifted her nose into the air like Rosie, and sniffed until she caught the scent of truffles—a loamy, damp smell that carried on the cold breeze, a scent most truffle hunters needed special dogs to detect. If she was quiet, if she listened and felt and tasted the air, she could find it. Calling out to Rosie, Nan followed the scent to a patch of wet lady ferns spraying out of the base of a fallen larch that had become a universe of moss and mushrooms. A Douglas fir towered nearby—the truffles grew symbiotically with the firs' root systems. She dug with her trowel and the freshly turned earth wafted up the fungal, animal-den smell.

"Don't tell me this is your retirement," a voice said. Nan looked up to find Clara sitting on the log. She hadn't heard her approach, but then she never did. Sometimes the only warning she got was a flash between the trees, Clara's elderly hunchback lumbering heavily through the blue woods, her yellow cardigan flashing between the conifer branches. Most times, Nan smelled her before she saw her: black loam, mycorrhizal webs, the sweet odor of rot broken down into soil.

She was sitting there, raising one stockinged ankle onto her knee and taking off her shoe to rub her knotty bunions.

"You oughta see yourself," said Clara.

"There's no shame in it."

"No one wants to see an old woman squatting in the mud."

Nan sat back on her heels, tossing the wisps of gray hair out of her eyes. "You're one to lecture me about aging gracefully. You've been wearing witch shoes and wool stockings since you were twenty."

"I seen Evelyn's home. What's your plan for them little girls?"

Nan sighed and shook her head as she dug. A few yards away, Rosie froze, growled at something in the underbrush, skin rippling between her shoulder blades. She shot off barking.

"I seen those awful McNealy sisters nosing around your place too. You remember when Myrna told me the reason she didn't invite me to her birthday party was because she didn't think my mother could afford a present? And I told her to go eat shit," said Clara.

Nan laughed. "I remember."

Clara put her shoe back on and set her foot on the ground. The bad foot, the one she'd injured skating on the lake as a girl.

It had never healed properly. She smoothed her skirt across her legs and a cloud of dust curled into the air.

"You gotta hide them girls. You can't let them nasty McNealy sisters see em."

Nan looked up again and saw Clara staring, her eyes deep and her skin translucent as a bridal veil, a universe crackling on the other side. Too big, too close—Nan looked away.

A still water silence settled between them, and Clara said quietly, "McNealys. Damn snakes."

The first soft, earthy lump rolled out of the soil and Nan snatched it up. "Ha!" She held it out to Clara, but Clara had already gone.

She didn't find many truffles this time—little more than a pound—but she carried them back to the car in the hammock she made with her sweater, dumped them into a plastic grocery bag she found in the back seat, and began the two-hour drive to Port Angeles. The Fox and Tortoise paid six hundred dollars per pound for the truffles. In good seasons, she could find five or six pounds of truffles and sell them to restaurants in Port Angeles, Whidbey Island, Oak Harbor, and Seattle. It was a decent supplement to the seven hundred sixty-three dollars she got from Social Security each month.

She used to sniff them out just for herself. Nan could walk through the woods around the lake and find them under the maples heavy with moss and ferns, under logs shelved with chicken mushrooms and liverwort.

The eastern sky was a bilious yellow-gray and Nan followed it all the way to Port Angeles, which smelled like sea air—brine and sand and dead fish. Rosie sat up sniffing. Nan rolled down the window so Rosie could stick her nose outside and suck in the air. The head chef of the Fox and Tortoise was smoking a cigarette at the back door—a young woman with a severe, glossy bun and an intense stare. She never stood up straight, shoulders slumping forward, which made Nan crazy.

The chef smiled a wan, joyless smile, and Nan could imagine that she was one of those women who didn't make herself smile or laugh in awkward social situations.

"You brought them?" the chef said.

Nan held out the plastic grocery bag. "About a pound."

The chef took the bag and led Nan inside. They went through the kitchen, which was quiet and clean with an antiseptic, metallic smell. The chef ran a disciplined kitchen.

She set the bag of truffles on a scale, which read out one pound three ounces, and then went to her office to calculate the sum, returning a moment later with $712.50 in cash.

Nan never lingered in town when she was making a transaction. Sometimes she drove five and a half hours to Whidbey Island or Oak Harbor just to get out of her car for twenty minutes, then get back in and make the return drive.

But this time, Nan took the money, folded it neatly in half, tucked it in her purse, and drove to the outlet mall. She left Rosie snoring in the car as she went into Sherman's Best to buy two car seats, a baby gate, outlet covers, and a high chair. She considered buying a crib, but she knew it wouldn't fit in the trunk with the high chair, so she set aside some of the money for later, when she could come back. Maybe a toddler bed for Lila too—though she doubted Lila would use it. She'd seen how the girl gripped Evelyn's shirt in her two little fists and panted into her neck while she slept. So she bought new linens for Evelyn's bed instead—something more mature than the bright-purple bedspread and matching pillows that were in there now.

The last time she'd bought bedding was when Evelyn came to live with her, when Nan found the skinny, fifteen-year-old runaway sleeping in an unused mop closet in the girls' locker room and she took her home, went to the store and bought her shampoo, deodorant, underwear. She'd called Evelyn's mother, Jube, to say, "I found Evelyn. I'm going to take her for a while"—even though she knew Jube hadn't been looking for her. She set Evelyn up in the guest bedroom, bought her a purple comforter and matching pillows, bought her a desk. She made her dinner every night and packed a lunch for her every morning before school.

But by then, Evelyn had been too used to roaming to settle into a life indoors, and she would come and go as she pleased, gradually staying out longer and longer until one day she didn't come home.

The high chair and baby gate were too bulky and the trunk wouldn't close, so Nan bought a black rubber bungee cord and looped the trunk halfway shut. It jutted up at a forty-five-degree angle.

She drove westward, under the heavy, low sky, skirting the grassy gorge that was once a prehistoric lake with long basalt pillars and a huge rock ledge that had been a four-hundred-foot waterfall. Beyond the waterfall, grooved within the high canyon walls, was a gully carved out by a thick, deep Ice Age river.

She used to teach Pacific Northwest geology, back when she was the high school's physical sciences teacher. Her students were bored, uninterested, except Evelyn, who couldn't spell to save her life, but who leaned forward on her elbows eagerly as Nan told the class about the geological soap opera of Cormorant Lake and the land around it—valleys cut into the cold, blue mountains by basalt floods and giant, sliding ice walls that picked up boulders on one continent and dropped them on another.

Cormorant Lake was the deepest lake in North America,

formed in the crater left behind by a huge volcano that had exploded nearly eight thousand years ago, as every child in town learned in grade school. The force of the eruption—which blasted up clouds of ash and pumice that traveled as far as the middle interior of Canada—had caused the mountain to collapse on itself. Pyroclastic flows boiled the surrounding mountainsides and river valleys, churning and sizzling all the way out to the ocean and incinerating the settlements of humans who had already been living there for three thousand years. The lake was so deep that you could submerge the entire Empire State building in its depths—so deep that when a train derailed in 1962 and rolled down the mountainside, it plunged into the lake, sank to the bottom with sixty-four of the town's residents inside, and was never found. No one knew whether it was the train that caused the landslide that buried the south shore the next day or if it was the result of logging and deforestation—loose, slip-sliding earth, no tree-root moorings to hold everything in place—but everyone blamed the train.

Only Nan knew that it was actually Clara. It was Clara's grief—her rage—that brought the mountain down.

As she drove on the narrow country road that wound through windy, moaning valleys and rolling blue pines, Nan got that lonely feeling that came upon her from time to time. She scratched her neck, feeling the old tracks left by her nails. It was something in the sharpness of the shadows, the raggedness of the trees, that reminded her that the ground was big and wanted her.

Winter was coming and the air was getting lighter, electric in its every-which-way current. Within the week, Evelyn had gotten two jobs: a night shift at the gas station, and a day shift at the country club. Between the two jobs and the time she spent replacing moldy drywall, the lack of sleep left her moving through the house in a bleary ghost glide. She fell asleep sometimes while she was talking to Nan—sitting on the couch, cartoons on TV for Lila, and Evelyn mumbling something about someone named Moose, and then she was snoring. Food was disappearing. Nan would hear Evelyn moving through the house in the night, and she wondered if Evelyn was eating whole loaves of bread and jars of peanut butter to stay awake.

Now Evelyn was striding across the room, tangle of hair flapping in her eyes as she picked up pillows off the floor and threw them on the couch, reached between couch cushions and pulled out wadded *Beauty and the Beast* panties. She held her hair out of her eyes with her fist. Such a waste of long, thick hair. Evelyn had never been able to appreciate it—the swing of it, the bend.

"What are you looking for?" asked Nan.

"My keys. I need to be at the country club in an hour. I should've been on the road by now," Evelyn gruffed, still holding her hair.

Nan moved behind her. She always kept a hair tie in her pocket, and she took it out and grabbed Evelyn's hair in both of her hands, yanking Evelyn's head back.

"Damn it, Nan! Not now!"

Nan didn't let go.

"If I had hair like yours, I'd treat it with more respect," Nan said, tying Evelyn's hair deftly before releasing her.

"Don't start."

"Well I haven't finished. Your problem is that you were born with good hair and you think it's always going to stay that way, but it won't. It'll get coarse and pubic and then you'll have to put some effort into it."

Evelyn didn't respond as she moved into the kitchen.

Mora wobbled after Evelyn and reached her fat, rolly arms up to her, bubbling *mamamamamama*. Evelyn swiped a hand over Mora's wispy hair before checking the top of the fridge again.

"Maybe they fell behind . . ." she was saying as Mora started whining—a fake, percussive cry—and hitting Evelyn's thighs with her splayed hands, wanting to be picked up.

Rosie had followed Evelyn and was sniffing underneath the fridge. Evelyn stepped on Rosie's paw, making the dog yelp loudly, which made Evelyn stumble back, bumping into Mora and knocking her down.

"God damn it," she whispered as she stooped stiffly to scoop up the wailing baby.

"You're not getting enough sleep," Nan said. "You don't need to be working so much."

Evelyn hugged Mora and looked at Nan over the baby's head, not saying what she wanted to say. Evelyn had always been good at not saying things.

"Sit. Hold your baby. I'll find your keys," said Nan. Evelyn, also good at taking direction, sat down at the table.

Nan checked the girls' usual hidey-holes, got down on her hands and knees on the living room rug like she was going to dig for truffles, and peered under the couch. There, she found all of the food that had been disappearing from the kitchen: the loaf of sliced bread now squashed and dusted with white fractals of mold, the plastic container of sandwich ham—dried out, curling at the edges—an open, oozing jar of peanut butter, a box of cereal, two bitten-into apples, and a set of car keys.

Nan left the food and brought the keys to Evelyn, who thanked her, looked up at her, and then looked away, never able to hold eye contact. Just like when she was little, when Nan would drive by the house on Greenland Drive and see Evelyn sitting cross-legged on the porch, eating from a box of cereal and wearing a sweater as pants, underwear visible through the collar at her crotch. So skinny. Pretending not to see the car, not waving back when she was waved to. When Nan stopped the car, Evelyn dropped the box of cereal and ran, disappearing behind the house.

By sunup there was movement on the rutted road. Nan pulled the lace curtains back from the front window as the McNealy sisters were walking their dogs up the hill with Mary Harding. The three old women were walking slowly, glancing furtively at the house, and Myrna was saying something to Mary Harding, whose penciled eyebrows were raised halfway up her forehead. Myrna and Helen were in their matching velvet zip-up robes and Mary Harding still had her hair pinned in curlers. Rosie, deep chested and balancing awkwardly with paws up on the windowsill, growled at the McNealy sisters' wispy little dogs.

"Little snoops, comin around to see if they can snatch a peek at Evelyn's love child," said Clara, who stood beside Nan at the window. "They heard there's a second one. Tryin to see for theirselves so they can go report back to Linney and Diane and Rhonda and the rest of them."

Nan narrowed her eyes at the gawking women and snapped her fingers at Rosie, who followed her to the front door. She opened it and Rosie shot out, barking. She shut the door and went to the kitchen to make another pot of coffee.

When Lila hadn't woken up by eight, Nan went into Evelyn's room to check on her and found Lila wheezing dryly in her sleep. Nan knelt and put her head on Lila's chest. No rattling. Just a tightness of the lungs.

She wrapped Lila in blankets and carried her out to the backyard, where the cold, damp breeze would clear her airways. She sat on the iced bench overlooking the flowerbed, stroked the hair out of Lila's face, tipped her head back slightly to open her throat. Nan sniffed. Lila's smell was off. Something had changed—something had gotten in.

Lila's breath came out in small, hot clouds that fogged in the morning chill. It took several minutes for the wheezing to ease and her breathing became clearer as she woke, frowning as her eyes focused. Nan took her back inside and set her down on a kitchen chair, handing her the toaster waffle that Evelyn had put out for her. There was always a plate ready for Lila to eat the moment she woke up so she wouldn't panic. Lila ate the waffle quickly—in another moment, it was gone. Nan opened the cabinet to get the honey, but it wasn't there.

"You got you breakfast, Nan?" Lila asked, saying "breakfast" as "beck-best." Nan hadn't known many toddlers in her lifetime apart from Clara's boy, Peter, but the word "beck-best" was, so far, her favorite thing about them.

"I'm looking for honey," said Nan, pulling out jars and feeling along the gritty high shelf.

"Honey?" Lila's voice was rough, gravelly.

"You're a little hoarse."

Lila pressed her hands to the sides of her abdomen, whispering to herself, "A little horse?"

Nan looked back at the couch. She went to the living room and got down on her hands and knees to pull out the bread, ham, apples, and peanut butter. And there was the honey bear squeeze bottle—empty, cap gone, a thin glaze puddled in its nose.

"Welp. That's okay, we needed to go to the grocery store today anyway."

The original grocery store had been buried in the landslide, and the new store was a squatty gray box with rust stains where the letters Whitman Union used to be—once a bank. Inside, the old fluorescents flickered weakly and the linoleum floor was sticky in spots. The cashiers were local kids, bored teenagers who whispered to one another, pointing at old Ida Greene, who always wore a bright-orange reflective construction vest because she was terrified of being hit by a car, or Ron, Ida's husband, who'd had a stroke some years back and now called girls "jeeps" and couldn't turn left when walking—making three right turns instead.

Nan put the baby in the shopping cart and tried to have Lila walk beside her, but the little girl moved slowly, fingers twisting together as she looked at the high shelves and the fire sprinkler pipes along the ceiling. Nan stopped and waited for Lila to catch up, but as soon as she started walking again, Lila fell behind. She put Lila's hand on the side of the cart and said, "Hold it." Lila shuffled alongside her to the condiment aisle to get the honey, and then to the meat section. While Nan looked at the chicken parts, digging to the bottom of the pile because the packages on top were always old and stringy, Lila let go of the cart and started wandering. Nan found her drifting like a hydra through the frozen-food aisle.

Mora started whining and grabbing at Nan's sweater. She usually went down for her morning nap at ten. What time was it now?

"Nan? We get this one?" asked Lila, pointing to a frozen TV dinner. She coughed a tight, wheezy cough.

"No, not today."

"We get this one?"

"No. Not this time. Come over here with me now."

Lila looked up at the tall refrigerators as she moved slowly toward Nan in the same distracted way Evelyn's own mother, Jubilee, had once wandered through the grocery store as a toddler.

Nan had known Jube since she was a baby. Jube's father, Royce, had been a small, fair man who made up for his womanly face with meanness. Her mother, Margaret, had been an outsider with a hard-boiled stare and a habit of dressing in men's trousers. She'd come from a company town that no longer existed, now just a ghostly scatter of outbuildings in the mountains. Jube, their only child, had been a fat toddler with a boy's haircut. Nan had seen Margaret and Jubilee in town, at the bank, at the post office—Margaret always walking three or four yards ahead as Jube tripped along absently after her, like a buoy bobbing behind a boat.

Nan thought of the time Margaret had walked through the grocery store as if she wasn't even aware that a child had followed her in—until she glanced over her shoulder and caught Jube gnawing on an unpeeled banana. Margaret took it from her, without heat or irritation, set it on a display of canned beans, and went back to her shopping. When it came time to check out, Margaret didn't have enough money, so she walked out of the store, leaving Jube behind, and crossed the parking lot to the bank. Nan had watched Jube toddle through the aisles, grabbing packages of snack cakes and pies and throwing them on the floor as the teenage bag boy trailed behind her, picking up the items and holding things she handed to him. When Margaret returned twenty minutes later, she matter-of-factly took the loaf of bread out of Jube's hands and set it on a box of laundry soap.

"What sweet little girls," said Linney Bradford as she approached Nan in the frozen-food aisle, hands dangling lizard-like in front of her as she smiled down at Lila. "I *heard* there were two!" Linney had never been good at disguising her snooping—not nearly as good as Myrna and Helen.

"How are you, Linney?" Nan asked flatly.

"Oh, you know. Puny. I can't seem to keep any weight on and the doctors don't know what's wrong with me. My granddaughter keeps giving me all these vitamins and things but nothing is working. I'm starting to wonder if it's worms. You know, Ida's grandson went to Mexico and came back with worms."

"Have you been to Mexico lately?" Nan asked.

"No, but I had coffee at Ida's house."

"That's not how you get worms."

"Well, you never know," said Linney. "How's your Evie doing?"

Behind Linney, Lila was calling to Nan. "This one? We get this one?"

"Evelyn is doing well," said Nan. "She's working right now—"

"Myrna and Helen said she got divorced?"

Nan looked at Linney, who was smiling too widely. She was trying to get Nan to confirm whether Evelyn had been married at all—whether the girls had been born out of wedlock.

Linney leaned in. "Myrna says to me, 'Our little Evie is back . . .' You know she always called her Little Evie—"

"I know."

"So she says to me, 'Little Evie's back with a little girl of her own, but Rhonda said she saw two of them, and would you believe Evie hasn't even been to see her folks yet?' And I says to her, I says, 'No, I just can't believe that.' And she says, 'It's true—hasn't been to see her folks yet and I don't think she—has—a—husband.'" Linney clapped her hands to punctuate the words. "And I says to her, 'No I can't believe that. Evie was never the kind of girl to do something like that. Nan brought her up better than that.' And Myrna says, 'But you remember Jubilee Rae and how she got divorced. Kids whose parents get divorced have all sorts of problems.'"

"Jubilee Rae got married when she was fifteen. Of course she got a divorce."

"This one, Nan?" Lila called out. "We get this one, please?"

Linney waved her dangling hands. "Well, that's just the

problem with the world today. People getting divorced, babies having babies and the like."

She looked at Nan and waited, eyes bright, expectant.

"Did Evie's husband leave the family?" Linney asked.

Nan sighed. "God damn it, Linney," she said as she grabbed Lila's hand and pushed the cart out of the aisle.

Nan was walking quickly, mimicking Linney's moon-eyed face to herself, and tugging Lila along, who was pulling back on Nan's hand and saying something in her fluid, breathless voice. Nan couldn't make out the words. "Nan—Nan, I just please—I have the please have the have the the—"

Nan went to the checkout counter and began loading the few items onto the belt. Lila was pulling on Nan's sweater while Mora whined and twisted in the seat.

"Nan I please have it the dinner with the rainbow and the bird and I hungry please I have it . . ."

"Lila!" Nan snapped in a whisper. "Stop that!"

Lila's face—pale as sea-washed bone—collapsed. She began crying long, wet sobs, and Nan tried to pull her in for a hug, but Lila went limp and dropped to the floor to cry facedown on the black felt mat. Mora whined in the shopping cart and twisted around. Nan bent over to pick Lila up—the girl wasn't heavy but her elongating bones were like swinging chains—and she dropped her purse.

"God bless America . . ." Nan hissed as she snatched her purse and hauled Lila up by the middle like a cat.

When she stood upright, she found Linney staring back at her, lizard hands hanging in front of her ribcage, smiling.

Nan threw her purse in the empty shopping cart.

"Fuck off, Linney," she said as she carried Lila and pushed the cart out of the store.

She left without any groceries.

As she drove out of the wet parking lot, she breathed in deeply to calm herself down.

"That was a bit much," said Clara, sitting birdlike in the passenger's seat—hands folded in her lap, shoulders rolled forward, head jutting.

Nan shook her head. "Linney's nosy. She was a nosy girl in high school, now she's a nosy old hag in the Spruce Tree Mobile Home Park."

"You gave her a good story to tell. Now they've got you in their sights." Clara straightened her sleeves and plumes of dust rose from her cardigan.

Nan sighed and looked at the little girls in her rearview mirror. Lila was crying quietly to herself with her hand in her mouth. Mora had already fallen asleep in her car seat, head slumped over on her shoulder.

"They always acted so nice but they never invited me to their parties," said Nan as she drove up behind a logging truck loaded down with huge, red, wet cedar logs.

"Maybe they would've if your mother had let you play with them as kids. Did you really want to go to their parties?" asked Clara.

"Of course I did. Everyone wanted to go to their parties."

The logging trailer was swaying slightly from side to side, drifting into the other lane. She tried to get around the truck, but it signaled to merge and she fell back. She cracked her window slightly to breathe in the sharp, clean cedar smell—wet wood and diesel fuel. On bright days, the smell of sunning cedars was dizzying.

"I always thought they'd start inviting me to their brunches and luncheons when I got married. Then I thought they'd invite me when I got pregnant," said Nan. She breathed in the sharp woody smell and thought of the day she returned to Cormorant

Lake after college to marry Earl, remembering the way the familiar heady scent of conifers and lake water had brought tears to her eyes—home. Not long after, Clara returned from a company town in Eastern Washington with a swinging baby belly and no husband.

"Oh, don't go getting soppy on me," said Clara. "You didn't really want to go to their parties."

"I thought maybe after everything with Peter . . ."

Clara turned to face her. "Look at me."

Nan did, waiting for Clara to say something reassuring, something about how they didn't need Linney and the McNealys and Mary Harding, but Clara didn't say anything, just held her stare—her eyes a mineral gray, the color of lake silt—until the blare of a horn and the flash of red brake lights lit up in Nan's face. She swerved onto the side of the road, just missing the stopped truck, and when she caught her breath, Clara was gone.

It was dark by the time Evelyn got home, slipping quietly through the front door and unlacing her boots without a word, eyes sweeping the room. Quarter past six and Lila was already asleep for the night, having skipped her afternoon nap. But Mora was still awake on the living room rug with Rosie, petting the sleeping dog's ears. When Mora heard the door, she pushed herself to her feet and toddled over to Evelyn.

"You're home late," said Nan.

"I know. Sorry," said Evelyn, pushing the lank hair out of her face as she stepped out of her boots. She lifted Mora onto the shelf of her hip.

"Just eat and get some rest," said Nan.

Evelyn ate little of her dinner—she'd never been able to put away much. Back when she was a teenager, they would go eat at the Chicken Shack on Fridays, and Evelyn always ordered an enormous plate of popcorn chicken but only ate three or four pieces before she started frowning down at her plate and picking at the pearly white C-shaped scar on her cheek, trying to work up the nerve to take another bite. At seven, Evelyn changed Mora into a nighttime diaper, brushed her four little teeth, and put on her sleep shirt. Evelyn kissed Nan on the cheek, said goodnight, and carried Mora to the bedroom.

There was something Nan was going to tell Evelyn, but what was it? Something about Lila? About Mora?

Nan always tried to wait long enough for Evelyn to fall asleep so she could go peek in at them, touch their hair and cheeks, maybe. But Evelyn was never asleep. At eight, Nan turned off the lights to go to bed, but lingered in the hallway to peer in the open door. Evelyn lay curled on the bed with her back to Nan, still in her jeans and sweater because she would have to leave for her night shift in a couple of hours. Mora's foot was propped up on Evelyn's hip, pink toes twitching.

Nan remembered the night fifteen years ago when she came out of her bedroom to find Evelyn in the living room, crouching on the arm of the couch and looking out the window at nothing, head tipped back so that the moonlight caught the bones of her egret throat. A caged bird trying to get to the night wildness. When Evelyn left shortly before her nineteenth birthday, Nan wasn't surprised. No note, no goodbye. Just an absence, a missing. Vanished with the car Nan had bought for her when she got her driver's license.

Now, Evelyn's body was curved into a comma, making a pause of herself around the little girls. Nan had once done the same thing for Peter—had made herself huge for him, big enough to hold the world on her back, and now she would make herself huge for Evelyn and her two daughters.

EVELYN

She almost walked into the bird: mangled, head dangling from a thread of skin, wings hanging limp, tail feathers fanned out in a death show. The bird appeared to be floating above her windshield, suspended in midair, but when she looked closer she realized that it had been impaled on a bare alder branch reaching over her car. That was how Evelyn knew Erin was coming for her—had already found her.

She'd come across the bird while walking to her car after her night shift at the gas station. As soon as she got over the shock—the grim acceptance that Erin was here—she grabbed a hamburger wrapper off the floor of the back seat, yanked the bird off the branch, and threw it in the trash can between the gas pumps.

She drove quickly out of the parking lot, scanning the trees—the bony aspens and alders, the shadowy firs—for Erin's staring eyes.

The drive to her morning shift on the north shore was an hour, and it wasn't until she stopped halfway at a topless diner called the Foxy Lady that she finally took her eyes off the rearview mirror. She got a cup of coffee and focused on the road for the rest of the drive, but she still couldn't shake the feeling that Erin was watching her.

The country club was a sprawling Spanish-mission-style structure with a clay-tile roof and rounded-arch breezeways. It jutted out of the mountain, overlooking the lake, and at night the blazing windows of the banquet hall were visible from the south shore. Lights winking across the darkness.

The club was situated among the north shore's historic Victorian houses, those of the railroad and logging families who had built the town, as well as the newer custom-built houses of the railroad and logging heirs: southern plantation, Dutch colonial, German half-timbered, all with long, twisting drive-ways and thick blue lawns.

She arrived at the country club at seven o'clock and unlocked the doors to the unlit aquatic center, the sharp cut of chlorine exhaling from the darkness as she felt for the light switch and flipped it on. Empty bleachers and plastic chairs sat around a still, aquamarine pool.

She'd been hired as a deckhand for the indoor pool, which held year-round swim lessons for kids. The job paid $8.75 an hour, which was fifty cents more per hour than the graveyard shift at Guthrie's Gas Station.

A week on the job and her car already smelled like pool water. She hadn't yet gotten used to the sinus burn of chlorine fumes and had to go outside every hour to gulp the clean, cold air. The smell drifted with her when she went home—stayed in her hair, her clothes. A chemical exhale. Nan's nostrils flared when they sat down to dinner.

But the work was simple and her mind could wander.

After she put her car keys and phone in the locker room, Evelyn turned on the water heater and cleared the traps of hair, bracelets, and barrettes. She added chlorine to the water, then cleaned the pool toys and scrubbed down the showers. The first lessons began at nine, and moms arrived in gym outfits, tugging grumpy toddlers.

By ten, she felt the sting of chlorine in her sinuses and went outside—eyes closed, head tipped back, throat open—when a deep, slightly too loud male voice said in passing, "You'll get used to it." When she turned around, she saw the wet hair and broad back of Jamie, one of the swim instructors, as he walked into the club, probably having just taken his break. His swim shirt and trunks were still wet and clinging. She watched the animal shift of his back and shoulders—fibrous, equine—not unlike Packy's sinewy leanness, thin but strong from doing drywall on construction sites. She'd felt it when she touched his shoulders, his neck, his back, feeling the humming kinetic tension under his skin. Packy would look at her, capillary waves shimmering in his eyes, when she ran her hands up his sleeves to touch his arms, or along the strip of pale skin above his waistband when his shirt pulled up. He'd smile at her apologetically, because being touched didn't come easy to him.

Evelyn went back inside the club. As she lugged five-gallon buckets of cleaning agents back and forth across the room, she stopped to rub her burning eyes.

"Looks like Miss Evelyn is sleepy. Maybe she didn't get her coffee this morning," said Jamie, startling Evelyn awake, as he guided a toddler into a back float. She looked at him and he glanced up at her, smiling. He didn't wait for a response, and released the toddler's head, yelling to the sinking boy in a sing-song voice, "Roll over."

She stood frozen, unsure of what to do with herself. She hadn't known she was being watched. Now she was aware of herself—of the way she was standing, shoulders rolled in lazily, body canting slightly to one side because she'd been planning to pick up the bucket, which would tilt her center of gravity. She walked away in a stilted, unnatural way, aware of the movement of her hips, her knees, the swing of her free arm.

In the remaining two hours of her shift, she bumped a hip into a doorframe. She dropped the squeegee three times before she was able to finally get the blade on the window. She went to wipe the hair out of her face and brought her hand up too fast, jabbing a finger into her eye.

By noon, she was exhausted, aching from the strain of trying to control her own body and its clumsy movements all morning. She would try to nap in her car before she went home.

She clocked out and crossed the parking lot, passing the loading zone where a box truck for Walden Farms Grass-Fed Beef was parked. The driver was waiting with a stack of boxes and a dolly. Evelyn recognized him by the way his head jutted out too far on his neck. She stopped, turned to go back inside, but it was too late. His eyes locked with hers and he smiled.

"Evie."

"Hi, Beau."

"Well, fuck me." He grinned widely. "I never, ever thought we'd see you around here again." He spoke with a loose-mouthed lisp due to the missing bottom row of teeth.

"You—look good," Evelyn said.

"Course I already knew you were here," he said, not hearing her. "Word's out you're back with a couple a brats in tow."

He laughed his big, expansive laugh.

"You're doing this now," Evelyn said, waving to the boxes. "You go straight then?"

Beau held his arms out—a big man, though not as big as she remembered, with a thick head of uncombed black hair, shaggy black eyebrows, and a beard that was patchy at the cheeks.

"That's me. Got clean eight years, three months, and four days ago. Now I eat too many sweets."

41

"I know what you mean."

She knew how drinking made you want nothing but salty and meaty foods, and how quitting made you suddenly desperate for sugar.

"I been having this problem with Pop Tarts lately. I wake up in the middle of the night to piss and go in the kitchen and eat two packs of em."

"Two Pop Tarts in the middle of the night? Every night?"

"Two *packs*. Four Pop Tarts. Every night. I need to get it under control, I know. Flo don't tolerate that kinda unhealthful eating, you know? She got me on vitamins now and she even bought a special blender to make smoothies . . ." He made a face.

"Oh. Flo," Evelyn said, smiling at the memory of the wide-hipped woman who used to drink with Jube at the kitchen table and brought her nail clippers with her every time she came over because she couldn't abide Evelyn's ragged, dirty fingernails. She would give Evelyn a peppermint to make her hold still while she clipped, pausing every few minutes to sip her beer or take a drag from her cigarette. "You and Flo, huh?"

"Yeah! Right after I got clean."

"She was always nice to me. Tell her I said hi."

"I'll do that." His smile slowly sank and he looked at her like he wasn't sure he should say what he was about to say. He coughed, snorted, spat a slimy wad into a puddle so that it floated, then said, "You should go say hi to your mom. She and Paulie still live over on Greenland Drive."

As she cut along the southern arc of the lake, a loud, tidal groan rattled the car windows—seeming to come from the sky, from the lake, from everywhere. The state sent out notices once a year to remind the people of Cormorant Lake that they were living on an active volcano. But no one worried about a volcano that hadn't erupted in over eight thousand years. The real danger was the landslides.

She took the long way home to drive past the mouth of Greenland Drive, wide and flat, arcing over the hillside and edging the gorge below. The road that she had cart-wheeled on as a kid, barefoot in her too-small clothes with split seams, pants that left her calcite-white ankles exposed, the dresses that fell just below the vertex of her pale thighs. She'd watch for the other children from the porch and they knew she'd be there. They'd yell to her and she'd run off to join them.

When the earth and sky rumbled and Katrina Meurer screamed theatrically, Cally Grohl said, "That's just the under-ground train." Pointing a finger at the ground they were standing on. "There's an underground lake and an underground train and an underground town."

No one believed her, so Cally showed them, leading them up the mountain road to an eastern ridge that looked out over the supine sprawl of the lake. She led them through the woods to a clearing, revealing a set of old, rusted train tracks. They followed the tracks—the splintering ties still smelling of creosote—to where they plunged into a grassy berm, as if the train that ran these tracks had simply dived down into the earth. They could see a clear downward curve to the rails.

"It goes all the way to the bottom," Cally said.

Evelyn got down on her hands and knees and listened, pressing her cheek to the cold steel, thinking she could hear the ancient squeaking of metal on metal, the grinding of gears, the roaring of the ghost train as it drew near—and underneath it all, somewhere down, down, down, the low, earthy groan of a monster.

When she got home, she went inside and found Nan in Evelyn's room in a chair under the window, rocking from side to side as she held Mora, who slept with her chin tilted up, mouth open, and one hand pressed to Nan's chest above her heart. Nan was smiling down at the sleeping baby. When she saw Evelyn, her smile deepened—grateful.

She stood up quietly and laid the sleeping baby on Evelyn's bed, barricading her in with pillows so she wouldn't roll off. When Nan came out of the room, she waited for the click of the shutting door to ask, "Lila's got a little bit of a cough. Have you ever taken them to a doctor?"

Evelyn paused.

"No."

"Lila is too small. She's skinny. Do you even know how old she is?"

Evelyn blew out her cheeks. "I don't know. Three, I think. She looked about two when they came to live at the house."

"I'll call them and see if they're open for walk-ins today," Nan said as she walked past Evelyn to the phone hanging on the wall in the kitchen. "You should be able to get in before they close."

The clinic was on the southeastern bend—a twenty-minute drive—high up on the hillside overlooking the town below and the lake beyond the pines, so still it looked like a sheet of cold metal. Old Victorians dotted the cliffs on the north shore, steepled mossy roofs rising out of the trees, white shingles glaring under a gray sky. The misty blue spruce and cedar treetops on the slope of the mountainside shook loose a cloud of crows that lifted and pulsed to the north, a dark scatter against the pale sky.

The trees on the south shore were the new growth after the landslide—when whole trees, ancient and enormous, slid with the loosened table of earth in one great heave, like the shrugging shoulder of a giant beast, into the iron lake below.

Nan had watched from the woods, standing between two egg-shaped basalt boulders, as the face of the mountain collapsed.

"And the sound," Nan would say. "A sound like the ground was waking up. Like the whole town had been built on the back of a sleeping giant." How many times had Nan told the story? "But what did they expect?" She'd touch her fingertips to her forehead then, as if to spool out the memory. "What did they expect?"

Evelyn carried the girls inside, one on each hip, Lila coughing lightly into her hair.

"Lila and Mora Winslow," she told the clinic receptionist.

"We have Van Pelt."

"That was a mistake. Winslow."

Nan had given the girls Evelyn's last name. But that was too risky, so Evelyn gave them Packy's last name: Winslow.

When the doctor came in to examine them, Evelyn only gave him the bare foundation of their history.

"A friend's kids. I'm taking care of them while she gets clean. They never been to a doctor before." She told something of the truth because the doctor didn't live on the south shore. Only one doctor had ever lived on the south shore: the surgeon, whose money built the clinic they were standing in now.

The pink-scalped pediatrician coaxed Lila to lie down and then palpated her belly. He helped her up again and listened to her heartbeat, her breathing, peered into her ears, eyes, nose, and mouth before looking at Evelyn over the rim of his glasses. "You said she's three?"

"I think she's three, maybe four."

"Did you know she has a six-year molar coming in?"

Evelyn stared at him, uncomprehending.

"That means she's at least five years old. How long has she been in your care?"

The words were a lead weight that hit her in the chest. Her ears were ringing. She had to blink the room back into place, and when it stilled, she saw the picture on the wall behind the doctor's head—the same picture on Nan's wall: the deformed toddler, confused with sleep—Clara's boy—and the severe doctor standing over him. A newspaper clipping framed beside it. Medical Miracle: Surgeon Adopts Patient with Rare Birth Defect.

"What?" she asked, realizing the doctor was waiting for her response.

"How long has she been in your care?"

"A—year. About a year," she said.

"Without a medical history, I can't be sure how malnourished she was to begin with, but depending on the severity, it will likely impact her in other ways as she grows. She may be cognitively impaired. I'll write you a prescription for a supplemental formula to get her weight up."

Evelyn's ears were still ringing as she walked the two little girls out of the doctor's office and into the parking lot, which was a greasy rainbow slick from last night's rain. They walked along the barbed wire fence that separated the parking lot from a marshy field of weeds, Mora on her hip, Lila gripping her hand tight as she stepped heel-to-toe along the cement curb.

She felt before she heard the groan of cracking bedrock echoing across the lake. She stopped and listened for the deep, tectonic breathing of a creature so large and ancient that massive cedars had grown right out of its back and whole rivers had cut tracks through its skin.

The next day, after her shift at the country club, Evelyn got in her car and drove the wet roads slowly back to the south shore and made a left onto Greenland Drive. She followed the road to where the pavement ended and turned into packed mud, rocky and pitted. The land had once been cleared for cow pastures, but now it was fields of waist-high cheatgrass and small, boxy houses. Particleboard duct-taped over windows, screen doors with the netting flapping open, holes rotting through roofs.

And there it was: the house where she grew up, the porch where Jube would leave her with a box of cereal, the front door that Jube would lock and refuse to open so that Evelyn would fall asleep sitting against it. Now the gable was rotting, and one of the two porch steps had fallen through with dry rot so the splintered boards stuck out like jagged tusks. A black trash bag had been taped over a broken window in one of the bedrooms, and cars and trucks without tires sat rusting in the grass like the shed husks of giant insects.

There was movement in the front window—a finger pulling down the miniblinds to look out. Evelyn kept driving. She'd eventually have to turn around and go back the way she came. They'd already seen her—Jube or Paulie—and knew it was her.

On her way back down Greenland Drive, she pulled onto the gravel drive strips and parked behind an ancient rusting Plymouth that looked as if it hadn't run in decades.

The yard was scattered with empty plastic flowerpots full of old, black water. There were at least two dozen because Jube was always buying plants, sometimes just snipping flowers from a ditch or the landscaped flowerbed of the bank.

She got out of her car, kicked the broken skeleton of a folding lawn chair out of her way. A cluster of beetles dispersed. Amid the moldering scatter of the yard, the air smelled sweet, like wood smoke and water.

The front door was open before she'd even reached the steps and Jubilee Rae Grimmley stood in the doorway in the same tinted glasses she'd worn throughout the '80s and '90s—a squat woman with teased hair, parted down the middle and fluffed to a warped yellow shag. Large, meaty arms folded over her chest. And no matter the weather, Jube could always be found in a T-shirt and jean shorts that fell just above her dimpled knees. It was forty-nine degrees outside. Above her, raggy cobwebs hung from the gable, full of crane flies and wasps and pine needles.

"We heard you were back in town," she said. "Come on in. Park yourself for a bit."

She moved aside and Evelyn stepped into the smell of cigarette smoke. The room had been steeping in it for years, windows closed, blinds drawn. The air was thick with dust and an archipelago of black mold was creeping up the wall behind the split recliner.

"I thought you'd've brought your girl around. Everyone's sayin you got a little one now. Sit down, sit down."

Evelyn sat on the dusty couch.

Jube took a pack of Camels out of her breast pocket and shook out a cigarette as she plopped down in the recliner. She tucked it between her lips and grimaced as she lit it.

"I gotta say, though." Jube exhaled the smoke and tilted her head down to look at Evelyn sternly. "It's one thing to hear through gossip that your child is back in town and didn't come say hi to you. It's another thing to find out your child's got a child and never told you."

Evelyn was silent.

Jube took a long drag and blew the smoke out into the room. The closed bathroom door was behind her and Evelyn watched it, remembering how it shook as the dog threw himself at it with a punching staccato of barks, full of rage. She'd stared too long into the dog's eyes, she was told. That was why he'd bitten her: he thought she was challenging him. Had she smiled? The dog would see that as a show of teeth—aggression. The scar started at the outer edge of her left eye and curved around her cheekbone.

The dog had been dead for twenty-five years. It was the closed door that made her chest feel tight. Open, it was a different door altogether.

"So Paulie's out there working at the lumber yard now," Jube said in a sudden, awkward way, taking a deep breath at the wrong time. "Full time, too. He's a general laborer in the warehouse. Got benefits and a week of paid vacation every year."

"Oh. Good. I saw Beau LaFevre yesterday. Looks like he's doing good. Says he married Flo."

"Yeah. Them two got married years and years ago. Beau and Flo." She laughed: a short, flat puff from her gut.

They fell silent again. Jube sucked on her cigarette, lips spongy with smoker's lines. She crossed her ankles in a languid way on the thin green carpet that was wrinkled and bunched in the spots where it had pulled loose. There were too many stains to tell the new from the old.

"Yeah, Irma and Roger made it official a couple a years ago. So did Willy and Cathy." Jube tapped her cigarette in the ashtray she'd set on the arm of the recliner. "Alvin got married last year. They moved to Spokane six months ago. His wife's dumber than a box of rocks, so we call her Rock behind her back."

Evelyn looked around the room, which felt like it was getting smaller, squeezing her out.

"So who's the daddy?" Jube asked.

Evelyn blinked, realizing that Jube was asking a question. "What?" she said.

"Your child's daddy. Who is he?"

Evelyn had never considered that question before.

"I—don't know," she said, because it was the truth.

"You don't know?" Jube said, followed by a flat *huh*, a joyless laugh.

Neither spoke, and Jube took a drag on her cigarette. When Evelyn didn't respond, Jube shifted uncomfortably.

"I just thought—well, I don't know what I thought," she said, waving her cigarette in front of her face.

"I should go," said Evelyn, standing.

"Yeah." Jube didn't get up from her chair.

Neither made a move toward the front door, but their silence was cut off by a loud report of barks that concussed in Evelyn's chest as the bathroom door banged and shuddered. Jube got up and hit the door five times with the flat of her hand.

"Duke! Get back in your bed!"

The store smelled rank. The hot dogs that had been rolling in the case all night had withered hours ago. As they turned on the metal rollers, sticky white threads pulled up with them and snapped. Soap. When Jan cleaned the hot dog case, she squirted an *S* of blue Dawn on a damp rag and wiped the hot rollers down without rinsing afterward. Evelyn could taste the mixture of cleaning agents and greasy hot dog drippings in the back of her mouth.

"The male flour beetle has little backwards spines on his tiny dick so that when he's mating with the female, he's actually removing the sperm left behind by her last partner," said Bobby Guthrie.

Bobby was the Guthrie Gas Station manager and the son of the owner. His long, overlapping front teeth gave him a rabbity look and his voice was that of a woman who'd been smoking and drinking all her life.

"The sperm of the male fruit fly has a tail that's two inches long. That's twenty times the length of the fly's body." Bobby was holding his thumb and forefinger four inches apart, eyes wide. "It's because when he mates with the female, she might already have a dozen other males' sperm in her body, and the sperm with the longest tails usually win. Do you know why human males produce so much sperm—something like a hundred thousand in a single drop? Why so many when there's only one egg, huh?"

Bobby Guthrie's family had come from the north shore. His father was a Stadler on his mother's side, but he was cut off from his inheritance when he married a waitress, so he used what money he had left to open the gas station.

"Why do you think that the human male evolved to produce millions of sperm each day when a female has only a limited number of eggs to be fertilized?" he pressed.

Evelyn looked at him. She'd tried ignoring him, tried pretending to be busy working—wiping the gluey black grime underneath the cash registers.

"I don't know, Bobby."

Bobby sighed and threw up his hands. "You're not thinking. It's because the male with the most sperm has the greatest chance of fertilizing the egg. If the female goes out and sleeps with four or five different guys in one day, who's going to get to the egg? The guy who blew the biggest load!"

"Bobby."

"My point is that it's all about competition. That's why the fields of business and economics are mostly run by men—I mean, there are a few outliers, some women here and there, but are there any Fortune Five Hundred companies run by women? Nope."

"I think there are a few," she sighed, rubbing her forehead. The skin felt grainy.

"No. There aren't," Bobby said, leaning toward her. "You know why? Because women aren't naturally competitive the way men are. Nature drives us to be competitive—to be the biggest, the strongest, to produce the most sperm, to cut our competitors at the knees. So when you have people like Hillary Clinton talking about 'workplace discrimination,' I just don't buy it. Women aren't as cutthroat as men are. They're not willing to get dirty, you know what I mean? They want stability. It's the way they evolved. They want a strong, healthy mate who will provide for them and give them strong, healthy offspring, so they tend to be not as invested in their work as men are."

Evelyn looked up at the clock. Five minutes left in her shift.

Lindy had called in sick, so Evelyn worked the night shift alone. Ten p.m. to six a.m. Bobby came in at five thirty, but he wrote five o'clock on his time card.

The gas pumps and parking lot were empty, and the morning drizzle was light and cold when she left, clutching her jacket tight around her neck. She wiped the wetness from her face as she got into her car, eyes dry as she started the long drive north.

Lila's cough was getting worse. No wheezing or phlegm, just a hard bark.

At least five years old. She should be in kindergarten then. It seemed impossible—she was no bigger than a toddler.

Evelyn, herself, had been a small child. The wild children with whom she'd played had been small for their ages too. But she'd never seen smallness like Lila.

She unlocked the country club pool and turned on the lights, put her things away, flipped on the water heater.

At eight o'clock, the office manager, Tanya, arrived, and then the first swim instructors clocked in at eight thirty.

Evelyn was walking back to the locker room to when she heard Jamie's voice.

"Morning, Little Miss McKenzie. Ready to swim?"

Evelyn watched from the doorway as Jamie took the hand of a goggled toddler in a pink two-piece and led her into the pool. He swished the little girl through the water and said, "Okay, ready? One, two, three—blow bubbles." And he dunked the toddler in the water.

When she came up coughing, goggles askew, he set her on the steps and bent down to adjust the lenses for her, his two hands nearly covering her whole head. He looked over the girl's head at her mother sitting in one of the plastic chairs on the pool deck. The woman was hugely pregnant, belly pulsing like a swirling blue planet under her Lycra athletic top.

"She's doing great, Mom," he said. "No crying this time."

And then he smiled at her—a dazzling, boyish smile that changed the geography of his face, opened it and made him flare with the heat and intensity of a newborn sun, collapsing the bellows of Evelyn's lungs.

She looked away, ducked into the locker room, took a moment to catch her breath. She went to the closet and got out the mop and bucket, some scrub brushes, and started scrubbing the showers. She worked through the rest of her shift feeling like electric plasma, like dendrites of heat and light arcing and snapping, charged by the energy of Jamie's smile.

She clocked out at noon and went to her car, but stopped when she saw Jamie with McKenzie's mom behind a silver GMC Yukon. He had her backed up against the SUV, his left hand hooked behind her right thigh, fingers creeping up the inseam of her maternity gym shorts as he kissed her.

Nan had once told Evelyn that human beings experienced pregnancy in a way no other species did because of the hemochorial placenta, which, at the moment of implantation, burrows into the uterine lining and rips open arterial walls to redirect blood flow to the growing embryo. The placenta then blasts open the surrounding tissues and pumps hormones into the arteries to expand them into newly opened spaces while paralyzing the mother's blood vessels so they can't constrict as they normally would at the prospect of bleeding to death. The placenta can then flood the mother's arteries with hormones to increase blood pressure, dilate her blood vessels, or make her blood sugar surge. And while most other mammals can opt out and reabsorb the fetus or expel it, the human mother is caught like a fly in a web.

"And do you know why all other animals can carry litters of twelve while hunting for food and running from predators? Or why they can give birth quickly and easily, while human mothers are left screaming in agony for days?" Nan had asked her. "It's because animals weren't meant to carry babies while walking on their hind legs. Pregnancy was never meant to be experienced standing upright, and the cost of our bipedalism and our great big brains in our great big heads is the single most painful and deadly childbirth experience in the whole animal kingdom. We evolved this way but that doesn't make it natural."

The woman's toddler was sitting in the back seat, pink rubber goggles still strapped around her head.

Jamie didn't see Evelyn watching, and Evelyn didn't make any effort to hide as the woman got into the silver Yukon and drove out of the parking lot. Jamie started back toward the pool entrance, and when he passed Evelyn, his eyes met hers and they were glassy with need. But then his face changed almost imperceptibly—enough to reveal that he knew he'd been seen.

At the country club the next day, Jamie didn't speak to her or meet her eyes. Evelyn did her work silently and watched him when McKenzie came in, watched as Jamie swam with her and said in his large voice that made no effort at smallness or containment, "Use your scoopers, Kenzie. Long, princess arms." When McKenzie wouldn't put her face in the water, Jamie got her a pair of goggles and Evelyn watched the muscles of his broad forearms shift as he put the goggles on the toddler and pinched the plastic lenses to adjust them on her chubby, smiling face, careful to keep the rubber strap from pulling her hair.

McKenzie's mother watched them with a smile—a secret smile that she and Jamie shared.

Tanya came out to tell McKenzie's mother something that Evelyn couldn't hear, and the woman pushed herself up from her chair with effort and followed Tanya back to the office, lumbering with the spread-hipped walk of the heavily pregnant, belly straining at her athletic top so that it rode up, exposing a strip of pale blue-white skin. Jamie watched her, entranced. Enamored.

After McKenzie's lesson was over, Evelyn found Jamie and Tanya in the break room, sitting at the table. Jamie was leaning back in his chair, eating a protein bar, his back to Evelyn, while Tanya was picking green grapes off a bunch. They were speaking quietly, and Evelyn watched them, half hidden in the hallway.

"Not much time left with Ursula," Tanya said. She plucked a grape, and Evelyn could hear the crunch of taut skin breaking open. "She's ready to pop."

Jamie didn't respond.

"I know things didn't work out so well between you and Sarah after she gave birth. I hear Grayson's mom is expecting," she went on, looking at him with a smile. "Just your type."

He ate his protein bar as if he hadn't heard her speak.

When Evelyn's shift was over, she walked out to her car, thinking about Tanya's words. "Just your type."

Her car was parked in front of a row of rosebushes and she got in and started it up, but stopped when she saw, directly in front of her, the shimmery green iridescence of a Japanese beetle. The beetle was impaled on a thorn—still alive, upside down, fading with a slow bicycling of its legs in the air. Erin had found her here too.

Evelyn looked around quickly, scanning the woods on the other side of the rosebushes—the larches and cedars and alders that crowded the perimeter of the parking lot—looking for a flash of coppery red hair, for a bony white hand sliding around a tree trunk.

She backed out of the parking space, hands clutching the wheel, and the Japanese beetle stopped moving—dead finally.

When she got home, Mora was crying at the table, twisting and hiccuping in the high chair. Her face was smeared with chocolate cake and her hair was glued to her cheeks with dried snot. As Evelyn unlatched the high chair tray, Mora's head swayed with exhaustion. She'd been crying for a long time. Evelyn lifted her out and Mora released a shuddering sigh as Evelyn carried her through the house, calling, "Nan?" Nan wasn't in her bedroom, the bathroom, or the girls' bedroom.

She carried Mora out to the backyard, feeling the baby settle her weight against Evelyn's chest—already asleep. She spotted

Nan, kneeling under the bigleaf maple that was dripping with moss. Her gloves and apron were smeared with mud, and she was clipping stems of stinging nettle and setting them aside in a basket.

"What are you doing?" asked Evelyn.

Nan looked up, frowning.

Evelyn saw that the soil had been turned in the flowerbed along the southern border of the lawn. The fresh earth smoked in the cold, steam curling around Rosie as she lay sleeping in the loam.

"How long've you been out here?" asked Evelyn.

Nan sat back on her heels and wiped the hair out of her face, leaving a smear of mud along her forehead.

"Oh, I don't know. I pulled the weeds in the flowerbed and planted some tulip bulbs. It seems like every year the blooms just get weaker and smaller, so I really have to replant every year—or at least every other year," said Nan. "I added a little fertilizer so hopefully in the spring they'll come up strong and bright."

Evelyn could feel the baby's breath, rhythmic against her neck.

"How long did you leave her in the high chair?"

Nan frowned again. The gray sky cast a silvery gleam over her eyes, made them look filmy. Evelyn could see Nan didn't understand what she was saying.

"Where's Lila?" Evelyn asked, looking around and realizing that she hadn't seen Lila since she'd gotten home.

She carried Mora back inside the house and went into the living room, where she found Lila folded up on the couch asleep, hands covering her face. Evelyn crouched down beside her and pulled her hands away from her face. Her breaths were tight, squeaking harsh, and her lips were blue.

"Shit," said Evelyn as Nan came in through the back door. "She's got pneumonia. Watch Mora."

She scooped up Lila, wrapped her in the afghan that was always draped over the back of the couch, and carried her out to the car where she buckled her into the car seat. Lila slept with her mouth open, slumped to one side on the drive to the doctor's office, and then she slept on Evelyn's lap as they sat in the waiting room, where two other women were already waiting. Two toddlers played with old toys on the floor while the women talked—women who didn't know each other, both young. One was little more than a teenager, with fire-engine-red dyed hair, heavy bangs swooping over one eye, nose and lip piercings, safety pins in her black clothes.

"Viper!" the teenage mother hissed, snapping her fingers at the curly haired girl who was throwing blocks. The girl looked up at her, smiling. She was wearing a *PAW Patrol* dress and leggings. She picked up another block and threw it at a poster of a woman breastfeeding. "Viper, stop it!"

The walls were covered in posters of mothers and babies: a poster of a mother in a nightgown holding a newborn, a poster of three quizzical babies lined up in a row, a poster of a pregnant woman cradling her belly.

"Winslow?" the nurse called.

Evelyn carried Lila through the door and into the hallway, where she had to wake her up slightly to set her down on the scale. Lila swayed, sleepily knock-kneed. After she was weighed and measured, Evelyn wrapped her in the blanket again and carried her into the examination room. They sat together in a small metal foldout chair in the corner, the blanket cocooning both of them, as the doctor came in—the same one as before.

"So Lila is having trouble breathing, huh?"

"Pneumonia, I think." Evelyn remembered when Jube had pneumonia, remembered her tight, rankling breaths, the blue tint of her lips, too weak to stand and walk, so Evelyn had brought her sandwiches and Pepsi. Jube gave her a five dollar bill and told her to go to the store and buy nicotine gum since she couldn't smoke, told Evelyn to bring back the change, but Evelyn—fourteen at the time—spent the rest of the money on candy. A year later, Paulie moved in and squeezed Evelyn out.

"Well let's take a listen."

Evelyn turned Lila around on her lap and the doctor pressed his stethoscope to her chest while she slept, mouth open like she was waiting for the Eucharist. The doctor listened, frowning, then peered with his flashlight into Lila's nose and ears. When he shined the light into her mouth, he flinched.

"Yep. That would do it."

"What?" asked Evelyn.

"She has pneumonia, but her tonsils are so swollen they're almost touching. See?"

Evelyn looked into Lila's mouth and saw the back of her throat, almost closed.

"Does she snore?" the doctor asked.

"She snores a little when she's real tired."

"We may need to talk about a tonsillectomy. But I would definitely want her to put on weight first."

The doctor opened a high cupboard and took out a machine—a small box with a hose and a plastic face mask attached. He called a nurse for a single dose of albuterol. A moment later, a woman in lumpy pink scrubs brought him a tray with a tiny brown vial. He poured the liquid—algae green—into the nebulizer cup, turned on the machine, and fitted the mask over Lila's face. As the liquid vaporized, it churned up the hose in a thick greenish mist that Lila breathed in. By the time the liquid was gone, Lila's lips had gone from blue to gray.

They left with the nebulizer, prescriptions for albuterol and antibiotics that she picked up on the way home, and a cash payment plan that Evelyn had no intention of paying.

When they got home, Evelyn carried Lila back to the bedroom where Mora was napping and settled her in the bed, lying down beside the girls. She took Lila's hand, rolling the limp fingers between her own, worrying the knuckles under the skin like river rocks. Evelyn used to carry small, smooth stones in her pockets when she was young, rubbing them with nervous consistency throughout the day—at her desk, at home, in her bed. She'd go into the school bathroom stall, take out the softest stone to smooth along her forehead, her eyes, her mouth.

She tried to sleep but she couldn't break the skin of it, skimming along the surface. When she gave up, she left Lila and Mora in bed and went out to the kitchen where Nan was drinking tea and reading.

She wanted to ask Nan what happened that afternoon, how she'd forgotten about the girls, but instead she asked, "You think the reason men produce so much sperm when there's only one egg is because of competition?"

Nan looked up from her book. "No," she clucked. "It's because the vagina is a self-cleaning organ that doesn't want anything in it. It's a deadly place where only the strong survive." She went back to her book, but then glanced up again. "You should get some sleep."

That night, after Nan had gone to bed, Evelyn sat at the kitchen table under the dim light bulb with her coffee and waited to start her shift.

The doctor had explained that pneumonia was fluid in the lungs. Evelyn saw Mora twisting in the bathtub, belching out bubbles like the toddlers Jamie swam with. She'd yanked Mora out, held the baby's small wet body to her own, and called to Packy, who'd been gone for weeks by then. When she remembered that he wasn't there, she felt hollowed out.

Sometimes he disappeared for days—sometimes for a week at a time, like Erin. On the days he disappeared, when he was nowhere, she slipped into his room and uncapped his deodorant, smelled it, swiped it on her own armpits. She found his toiletry bag and took out his toothbrush and brushed her own teeth with it using his Colgate toothpaste. She went through his dresser drawers and put on his clothes—his Hanes boxer shorts, his worn-out jeans that were too tight on her hips, his ratty work T-shirts that always carried a tinny sweat smell even when he'd just washed them. She'd lay in his bed in all of his clothes, stewing in the metallic smell mixed with the laundry detergent in his sheets, wanting to live in it.

In the three years they'd lived together as roommates in Doris Clearwater's house, they'd never shared a room, not even when Evelyn was crawling into his bed every night. They were two parallel lines traveling at a constant speed, side by side, never bisecting.

And then she saw the skinny toddler in the backyard, fault lines of blue veins in her eye sockets, cramming handfuls of orange honeysuckle flowers in her mouth.

After Erin left, Lila and Mora slept in Evelyn's bed, Lila pressing her whole body against Evelyn, the baby snuggling down between the pillows before Evelyn learned that she could smother that way. She made bottles before she went to bed each night so that when Mora woke up at midnight—then two a.m. and then four a.m.—Evelyn could just grab one and pop it in the baby's sucking mouth. In the dark, Evelyn would walk her fingers along Lila's curved, amphibious spine—her bony beginnings—feeling the vertebrae the way she used to roll her thumb over a frog's spine to find the hidden architecture inside.

She didn't slink into Packy's bed so much. A coolness had settled between them. A distance—undefined. Evelyn couldn't find its edges, didn't know where it began or ended. She knew Packy was uneasy in their new silence.

It was his idea to leave.

Erin had been gone for almost a year and Evelyn and Packy started making plans. They would pool their money together. They would take the girls with them to Butte. He'd wanted to leave, get out of Riverside—it was a dump, all smog and flatland dust—go to Montana, with its big reach of sky and hills spinning out to new universes. Some friends of his had gone there and said it was perfect: a mix of town and country, and lots of space and space and space.

And then Erin came back and Evelyn said to him, "Just wait. Just wait a little while." And he said, "For what? For her to leave again? She's their mother. What did you expect?"

But she couldn't leave them, and the next day, Packy was gone. He didn't wake her before he left. He didn't leave a note.

Now, Evelyn stood and went to the hallway to see if Nan's door was open, like she used to when she was a teenager, when she would peer in to find Nan asleep on her side, balanced on the axis of her wide hips, sometimes just napping during the day with her feet delicately stacked, the seams of her pantyhose crossing over her toes. But Nan had finished reading and her light was out. Evelyn listened. The faucet was dripping—a slow, ponderous drip. She went to the sink and twisted the knob tightly shut, but the faucet kept dripping. It would need a new set of seats and springs.

A movement outside the window caught her eye—a body flashing through moonlight—and she saw the flicker of red hair, a bony elbow, a bare shoulder gleaming lunar blue before rolling backward into the shadows.

Evelyn caught her breath and lurched away from the window. Her blood vessels tightened and throbbed in her temples as she ran outside and shouted her name.

"Erin!"

The ferns and pine spray rolled in the moonlight, but there was no other sound. Evelyn looked at the road behind her. Empty. No car, no Erin.

Wiping the cold sweat from her forehead, she went back up the porch steps. She didn't see the bird on the door until she was turning the knob—but there it was: headless, twisted, feathers savaged, pierced through with the tiny nail that Nan kept in the door to hang her Christmas wreath on every year.

NAN

Lila's smell was off. Sour. So Nan packed up her gardening tools and wrapped them in her apron. She would go to the woods to strip the bark off an elder tree. She would dry it, grind it, steep it into a tea, and put it in Lila's sippy cup.

But there was a knock on the front door. She opened it and found Myrna's husband, Terry, on the porch with a smile.

"Thought you might like some help patching up that roof. Evelyn's got enough on her plate being a single mom with two jobs, and with a little sick one," he said, scratching the loose skin of his neck so that his fingernails left dry tracks. Handsome and popular in high school, he'd aged slightly better than Myrna, in that he was still capable of standing up straight and his teeth were smooth and white like the rim of a bone china plate. He'd gone as jowly as the rest of them and his scalp and hands had become speckled with liver spots. But he was still getting up on roofs at eighty-two.

While Nan could expect the worst in people, she'd always had a difficult time *assuming* the worst, and she said, "Thank you, Terry. That's very kind of you." She didn't ask how he knew

Lila was sick. She didn't have to—Myrna and Helen would've already known somehow.

Terry smiled the same boyish open-mouthed smile he'd flashed in his yearbook photo and trotted down the porch steps to get the ladder off his truck. He was up there on the roof when there was another knock at the front door. Nan opened it to find Clara on the doorstep in her yellow cardigan and brown skirt, a hard lake wind at her back.

"What are you doing letting him up on your roof like that?" she asked flatly.

Nan looked up and down the rutted road and grabbed Clara's arm. "Get in here before someone sees you." She shut the door behind Clara and wiped the dust off her hands. "He offered and I accepted. What's wrong with that?"

"You know exactly what that old goat is after."

"That's your problem, Clara. You always think everyone is up to no good. What if he really wants to help?"

Clara looked at Nan in humorless disbelief.

"You really think he dragged his old ass over here just to patch your roof?" Clara asked. "You still got a crush on him?"

"Shh!" Nan shushed, hands out, as if someone might hear. "Don't you start. I am not sixteen years old. I don't have crushes."

Lila's tight, barking coughs cut the women off and they both looked at her where she lay curled up in a nest of quilts on the couch.

"I can't stand here and argue with you right now, Clara. I need to go find some elder bark," said Nan as she went to the couch, wrapped Lila in a quilt, and picked her up.

As Nan carried Lila out to the car, Clara stood in the doorway, arms folded over her sunken chest. Nan settled Lila in the back seat and went back in for Mora, picking her up off the floor and carrying her to the car.

"Where you off to?" called Terry.

Nan spun around, quilt feathers floating off of her, and looked at Clara on the front porch, and then up at Terry.

"Just running some errands," she said.

"You don't need to take the little ones there. I can go get whatever you need," Terry said, gesturing at the car with his hammer.

"Oh, no. I just have to gather a few things for the sick one." Ignoring Clara's pointed glare.

Terry chuckled—a puffing, knowing laugh. "Making one of your brews? You still doing that?"

"Bye, Terry!" Nan called as she got in her car.

Nan steered down the steep road and the Crown Victoria bounced as gravel pinged against the undercarriage. Lila dozed and Mora slapped her hand against her window and babbled as Nan drove the half mile to Linden Lane: once a driveway, now an overgrown trailhead. A rusted green gate blocked off the lane. Nan parked and got Mora out of the car, leaving Lila asleep in the back seat. Carrying Mora on her hip, she edged around the gate and walked a few yards up the lane before stepping off the trail into the wet ferns, following the shallow rise to the ravine on the other side, where a constellation of wild elderberry bushes grew—the descendants of the ornamental bushes that the surgeon planted along the lane decades ago to screen off visibility of the house from the road. She'd walked up that lane a lifetime ago, seeing the sprawling house as it flashed through the gray elderberry branches and rhododendrons. Now the house was rotting away, and the old greenhouse with it—both just roosts for owls and bats—not that Nan ever walked as far out as the greenhouse, where crowds had once gathered to see the Boy Without a Face for a dollar apiece.

Nan set Mora down in a patch of grass as she got out her

pocketknife and carved chunks of bark out of the elderberry branches. She yanked handfuls of leaves and stuffed them in her pockets with the bark, remembering how she'd once followed Jube's mother, Margaret, out to the lake to find her kneeling in the icy mud. 1972. Jubilee had been absent from school for over a week. She was six, in the second grade, not because she'd skipped but because Margaret had started her in kindergarten at the age of four. No phone call or note from the doctor. Calls to the house were going unanswered. Nan—then the elementary school nurse—was sent to check on the family since she lived right across the road from them, close enough to hear their screen door slap shut. Close enough to peer out her front window and see boot prints leading into the woods behind the house.

Nan had followed her to the lake, hanging back as Margaret pulled her canvas jacket tight around her narrow hips and stepped carefully into a wide puddle of ice slush, steeped black with old leaves. Her boot sank up to the eyelets and her dark hair—fine, thin, long—fell in a curtain over her face.

Gray sky and fog, snow banking the lake but the water not yet frozen. Margaret used her boot to turn over the ropy, frozen twist of a dead trout. She knelt and drew a small cloth from her pocket, holding it open with one hand while she picked at the skeleton with her other and placed something in the rag. She picked at the skeleton four times before folding up the cloth and tucking it into her pocket. She stood up and wiped her hands on her trousers before trudging through the snow, back the way she came. Nan followed her through the woods, back to her house, where Margaret disappeared inside. Nan walked up the front porch steps, opened the torn screen, and knocked on the door, the bottom of which had long been scored by dog paws.

She hadn't seen Jube in days. Most afternoons, the thatch-haired girl was locked outside, a box of cereal left on the front porch in case she was hungry. When Jube got thirsty, she drank from the hose, and sometimes she napped on the porch steps. If she had to go to the bathroom, or if the weather was bad, she came to Nan's house, and Nan made her lunch, let her watch TV on the couch—but Jube never stayed long, always leaving after finishing her sandwich or her cartoon and running back to her own yard without saying goodbye or thank you or even turning up her hangdog mouth in a smile.

Nan knocked again but there was no answer. She waited, listening to the murmuring coming from inside.

"Margaret?" she called, knocking.

The talking stopped.

"What? Nan? What do you want?" Margaret called back, her voice close, as if she'd pressed her face to the door.

"The school asked me to check on Jubilee," Nan said.

There was silence. No deadbolt sliding or lock clicking open.

"Jubilee Rae is fine. Just a fever," Margaret finally said.

"You need a doctor's note," said Nan. "The school is going to call child services if you don't get a doctor's note."

Nan waited, but Margaret didn't say anything.

"If you let me see her, I can let the school know she's okay," said Nan.

A moment later, the deadbolt slid open. But the door stayed closed, and she heard Margaret's footsteps walking away, so she tried the knob and pushed the door with a shove because it was swollen shut.

The house was choking hot and muggy, the thick smell of broth heavy in the air as steam from a boiling pot in the kitchen fogged the windows. Margaret was lowering herself onto the arm of the couch, above Jube's head as the girl lay sleeping on top of a heap of clothes, head tipped back and mouth open. Her face and neck were shining with sweat, and the chest and armpits of her little white undershirt were damp.

"How long has she been like this?" Nan asked as she stepped toward the couch.

Margaret didn't answer as she drew the cloth from her pocket.

"Have you taken her to a doctor?"

Margaret ignored her and opened the cloth. Nan couldn't see what was in it. She stepped closer and waited for her eyes to adjust to the dim light. Margaret picked at the cloth, pinched something between thumb and forefinger, and Nan could see it, thin and wriggling, glistening—a maggot. Margaret turned Jube's head to one side and then dangled the maggot over the sleeping girl's ear.

"No," Nan gasped, hand out.

Margaret looked at her, eyes hard, but without heat. The same dispassionate stare she'd turned on Jube in the grocery store years earlier.

"Will you take her?" Margaret asked.

Nan felt her mouth bob open and shut. "What?"

Margaret stared until Nan finally stepped back. She lowered the maggot into the whorl of Jube's ear canal and it disappeared. She took a wad of Kleenex from her pocket and tucked it into Jube's ear before turning the sleeping girl's head over and dropping another maggot into her other ear. She folded up the cloth and tucked it inside her pocket before looking up at Nan.

"They'll eat the infection," said Margaret. "She'll be better in the morning."

And she was right. Jube was back in school two days later, ashen, gums pale and receding so that her long teeth gave her a horsey look that would stay with her for the rest of her life.

A few weeks after Jube returned to school, Margaret would disappear, leaving behind a pair of men's pants and a flannel shirt laid out on her kitchen floor, with her wedding band where her hand would've been and a pair of earrings where her head would've been, as if she'd simply fallen backward through the floor.

When Nan got home, Terry was still up on the roof and Myrna was waiting on the front porch with a casserole dish and a smile.

Nan carried Mora up the porch steps and let Myrna follow her into the house. She gestured to the fridge and let Myrna rearrange the shelves of food while Nan went back out for Lila. By the time she'd gotten both girls settled—Lila in her nest of blankets on the couch, Mora in her high chair for lunch—Myrna had taken a seat at the table and was waiting for Nan to offer her coffee or tea. Nan stomped into the kitchen and put on a pot of coffee.

Clara would be furious right now.

Nan came back to the table with two plates of the teacake she'd made the day before. They sat in silence as they sliced into the cake, which had lost some of its moisture overnight—and if anyone would notice a dry cake, it would be Myrna Brzezinski. Myrna took a bite, swallowed tightly and paused, looking around the table, and Nan realized that she hadn't put out water, so she got up and filled the glass carafe at the tap. She brought it to the table with two empty glasses and Myrna filled hers as Nan went back to the counter to get the coffee.

"What do you think of this apple cider vinegar thing?" Myrna called. "It's supposed to be good for colds."

"Hmm?" Nan glanced over her shoulder at Myrna. "Cream but no sugar, right?"

"A little sugar," Myrna said with a smile, thumb and forefinger pinched together.

Nan brought the cream and sugar to the table in her grandmother's bone china creamer and sugar bowl, before going back for two mugs and spoons. When she finally sat and poured the coffee, Myrna asked, "Did she go to that Doctor Kipling?" nodding her head toward Lila on the couch. "That man doesn't know his elbow from his asshole."

Nan laughed, forgetting herself for a moment, and through her half-closed eyes she thought she saw Clara's face behind the lace curtains, frowning at her, but when she caught her breath and opened her eyes, Clara was gone.

"He had Mary's four-year-old granddaughter walking around with strep throat for weeks before he finally thought to test for it," Myrna added. "She got antibiotics, and wouldn't you know it, the strep cleared up in a few days." Her eyes and mouth popped open in mock surprise.

Nan shook her head and they ate their dry cake in silence.

"You were always a lifesaver for us mothers, when we had little ones with fevers and coughs that the doctor couldn't help us with," said Myrna as she spooned sugar into her cup.

Nan sipped her own coffee as Myrna's words swam around the room like a salamander. *Us mothers*. Referring to herself and Helen, Linney, Mary.

"Do you remember what it was like to have a child with the stomach flu?" Myrna asked. "When they couldn't keep anything down and went white as a sheet while their fever climbed? And the doctor's office simply said you had to wait it out?" She shook her head and sipped her coffee, and Nan looked at her, studying her face over the rim of her own mug. Myrna didn't return the stare, didn't seem to be aware of the gulf between them—the fact that Nan wouldn't remember what it was like to have a child with the stomach flu.

Myrna sighed and said, "It was such a relief to be able to go to your house and get one of your homemade medicines. Something that would just ease their discomfort a little." She looked at Nan and took a bite of her cake. "What are you giving Evie's girl?"

Nan set her cup down and hesitated before saying, "A little elder bark. It's an astringent so it should clear some of the fluid. But I doubt she'll see much improvement without stronger antibiotics."

Myrna nodded. "We're lucky to live in an age of antibiotics."

Nan made a noise of agreement.

"They're beautiful girls," Myrna said, nodding at Mora, who Nan had somehow forgotten was sitting right next to her. "They must have gotten their father's looks. They certainly didn't get that red hair from Evelyn."

A saucer fell off the kitchen counter and Nan jumped, knowing without needing to look that it was Clara—reminding her.

Nan stood up. "I'm so sorry, Myrna, but I should put Mora down for a nap and give Lila her breathing treatment now."

"Of course, of course. The casserole just needs to go in the oven for half an hour at four-twenty-five. Let me know if there's anything else I can do to help."

"That's so kind of you, Myrna."

"Oh, it's nothing."

Myrna left with a smile, and Nan scowled and lifted Mora out of her high chair. She carried her into the living room and set her on the floor to play while Lila went on dozing on the couch, which was where both girls were when Evelyn came home after sundown. She walked through the front door with one finger pointing at the ceiling.

"Why'd you pay someone to do the roof? I was gonna finish it this weekend," she said while shrugging off her jacket. "And he did a shit job. Don't pay someone to fuck up the roof."

"Evelyn Van Pelt—"

"Just don't throw your money away on someone who don't know what he's doing. I'm gonna get to it, I just have . . ." She finished her thought by throwing up her hands.

Nan pointed a knuckly finger at Evelyn.

"Evelyn Van Pelt. I understand you're exhausted, but you will not walk in here and start telling me how to see to my own house. Terry Brzezinski came by and offered to help, since everyone knows how much you're working these days."

"Terry Brzezinski?" Evelyn said, pausing as she unlaced her boots. Nan went to the entryway and held out her hand for Evelyn's boots as she took them off. "The Terry Brzezinski that told Sally McMahon that the reason her son is a tweaker is because she worked when he was little instead of staying home with him? The Terry who told Norma Finkbeiner that she's getting porky—at her mother's wake? That Terry Brzezinski came over to patch the roof? For me?"

"Oh, stop. He's not all bad," said Nan, taking Evelyn's boots out to the garage and setting them on the top step to air out, just as she used to do with Earl's boots. When she came back into the living room, she found Evelyn folded over Lila on the couch, a closed oyster, arms and hair draped over the sleeping toddler so that Nan couldn't see their faces. Evelyn whispered something to Lila, who didn't move. They stayed like that for several minutes until finally Evelyn sat up and rubbed her eyes, a recent cut flaming on the knuckle of her middle finger. Her hands were chapped red—just like Earl, she didn't take care of her hands. Nan used to have to rub lotion onto Earl's hands while he was sleeping, taking special care to massage the tight, shiny skin of his right hand to try to loosen his fist.

"I'm going to try to nap before I go to Guthrie's," said Evelyn, eyes still closed as she rose stiffly from the couch.

Nan opened her mouth to say, "I'll feed the girls," but stopped when Evelyn turned around, scooped up Lila in all her blankets, and carried her into the bedroom.

Evelyn always went straight to the country club after her night shift at the gas station, so Nan had gotten used to waking up with the two little girls just before sunrise—Mora seeming to wake at the exact same moment as Nan so that when Nan opened her bedroom door, Mora was already waiting in the hallway, splayfooted, heavy head craned back to stare up at Nan in the darkness. Every morning, Nan yelped and clutched her heart.

Now she hefted Mora onto her stiff hip and carried her into the girls' bedroom, where Lila was curled on her side, facing the wall, the same way Evelyn slept. Nan set Mora down and listened to the baby's arrhythmic footsteps stomping out of the room and down the hall as Nan bent over—a sharp red pain flaring in her lower back—and scooped up Lila. She carried the sleeping girl in all her blankets into the living room and settled her on the couch, pausing briefly to press a hand to Lila's forehead before going into the kitchen for a tiny single-serving vial of albuterol. She brought it back to Lila and set up the nebulizer on the coffee table, pouring the albuterol in the cup attached to the mask and starting the machine. She strapped the mask to Lila's face and Lila's eyes opened briefly—unfocused, prismatic—and then shut again. Nan went to the piano to play for the two girls:

Debussy, Clair de Lune. Mora toddled over and leaned against Nan, resting her head on Nan's knees as she played until the window light brightened to a spectral gray, and she remembered a time when she did this exact same thing with Peter, when he leaned his heavy head against her, sleepy, hair flurrying everywhere while she played.

A hard knock at the door made Nan and Mora jump. Nan glanced at Lila briefly, seeing the little girl's breath fogging the plastic mask, before standing and opening the front door. A smiling man stood on the doorstep, nice enough in khakis and a red gingham shirt collar poking out of his cashmere sweater.

"Nancy Woodrell? My name is Tom Parker. I'm with the Department of Social and Health Services." He lifted his clipboard. "I understand you have two young children in the home?"

An itch spidered up Nan's spine. "Yes."

"We received a call and I wanted to stop by to see how they're doing."

Nan blinked, the words processing slowly. "Someone called you? About us?"

"Yes, and I'm sure you understand that we have to investigate every report we receive." He raised his pencil.

"A report? Someone reported us? For what?"

"May I come in?"

Nan opened her mouth as she tried to think of what to say, but finally stepped aside to let him in. The man, youngish with a full head of hair but the beginnings of a sagging belly, stepped past her and looked around the room, making no attempt to hide his appraising stare the way a woman would, sneaking furtive glances when the hostess had her back turned. He looked around the house, at the cobwebbed corners, at the old sleeping dog on the rug, at the little girl wadded up in blankets with the nebulizer mask strapped to her face. He wrote something on his clipboard. He didn't ask if he could open the cupboards or pantry before doing so. He opened the fridge and bent down to inspect the shelves.

"Are you going to turn on the oven and make yourself a roast?" Nan asked, crossing her arms.

The man glanced over his shoulder at her and smiled patiently before closing the fridge and opening the freezer, flinching as a bag of chicken nuggets fell out and landed on his feet. He wrote something on his clipboard.

When he'd inspected the bathroom and bedrooms, he came back out to the living room and knelt beside Lila, searching her face for a long time. Nan tensed her thighs, her abdomen, ready to lunge if the man tried to wake Lila, but he didn't. He turned his smile on Mora, who was watching him with a frown like she smelled something bad, and he fluttered his fingers on her neck to tickle her. Mora jerked away, her frown deepening.

The man rose to his feet, making another note on his clipboard before asking, "How long has she been sick?" gesturing with his pencil at Lila.

"About a week," said Nan.

"And you've been to a doctor?"

"Where do you think we got the nebulizer?"

The man wrote something on his clipboard.

"And you've been administering the medication as the doctor prescribed? You haven't been supplementing with potentially dangerous holistic medicines?" the man asked.

"Holistic medicines? What in God's name?"

"Herbs that might be toxic to children? Plants?"

Nan felt a tightness in her lungs, a compression of her ribs. Her scalp prickled hot. Myrna.

"No," she said.

The man smiled and made another note on his clipboard

before saying, "Thank you, they look well cared for. We'll call you if we have any concerns to address with you." He let himself out.

Nan watched from the window as the man got into a dirty and dented white Ford Focus that was parked at the end of the slush lawn, made a three-point turn in the muddy, rutted road, and then drove back down the hill. When he was gone, she dressed the girls in sweaters and carried them one at a time to the Crown Victoria. Rosie trotted out with her, hopping in the back seat to lie on the floor beneath the girls' dangling feet. Nan made the drive down the road and around the corner to the Brzezinskis' house, trying not to think about how she shouldn't. Trying not to think about how she should be keeping the girls hidden from sight—from social services, from her neighbors, but most of all, from Myrna. And yet there she was, parking in front of the house just as Myrna was coming outside in her god-awful zip-up robe, with her cotton ball dog on a leash. Helen was with her, faint and shrinking with her tucked chin, and it was Helen who spotted Nan first as she got out of the car, leaving it to idle in the street.

"What do you mean by calling social services on me, Myrna Brzezinski?" Nan called.

Myrna paused, eyes on Nan, her face an arrangement of feline disinterest. Annoyed, almost.

"Good morning, Nancy," she finally said, straightening her back. "I hope you enjoyed the casserole."

"Hardly. And I had reasonably low expectations."

Myrna's eyes narrowed.

Nan took a step toward her. "Where do you get the gall to come into my house, eat cake and drink coffee at my dining table, and then call social services on me?" she asked. Her shoulders were tightening and she could see it like something wolfish, the muscles gathering for a burst of carnivorous power.

"I called out of concern for those poor little girls. You have no business digging up weeds and feeding them to children to see what works, like they're little lab experiments—and taking them into the woods when it's forty-five degrees outside and they're sick. But that's your problem, Nancy Woodrell. You always thought you were smarter than everyone else," said Myrna, hands on hips as her little dog yapped and hopped, plucking at the leash on her wrist. "Sitting there in Miss Reinholt's English class, telling everyone that Walt Whitman was *the first great American poet*." Myrna batted and rolled her eyes mockingly.

"He was!" Nan shouted, knotty fingers clenching and unclenching at her sides. "'Song of Myself' was the first poem to celebrate the central ethos of American individualism!"

Helen puffed out a derisive laugh, looking at the ground and covering her mouth.

"His poetry is just a lot of self-absorbed whining!" Myrna shouted.

Nan made a noise—a squawk that came from somewhere in the cavity of her gut—and then she was stomping toward Myrna, hearing herself mumble *bitch* as she took off her earrings. Myrna grunted and scrambled up the walkway and inside her house with Helen in tow, screen door banging shut on the leash as she tried to yank the dog inside. Helen opened the screen, dragged the dog inside, and slammed the door shut. The McNealy sisters were both inside with the deadbolt locked, and Nan was standing alone on the lawn, panting and looking around at the neighbors that had come out of their houses to watch the fight. There was Ida Greene in her reflective-orange safety vest. There was Beau LeFevre in his stained sweatpants and long hair. There were Linney and Mary, walking toward the house with their own dogs, pausing big-eyed at the sight of Nan on the front lawn.

And there was Lila, slumped over in her booster seat with her oxide red curls covering her face, and Mora, sitting upright in the driver's seat because she'd somehow maneuvered out of her car seat straps. Both girls' red hair and ultraviolet skin made them visible to everyone on the street.

Nan went back to the car, opened the driver's-side door and pushed Mora across the bench seat to the passenger's side. She buckled the seatbelt across the baby's body and drove back up the hill, deciding that she wouldn't tell Evelyn about the visit from social services, or the confrontation with Myrna—because Evelyn would worry. She'd lose even more sleep. But Nan wondered how long it would take for the news to get back to her.

EVELYN

Ursula led McKenzie to the pool, and when Jamie saw her, he broke into a wide, boyish smile—unabashed joy. Evelyn watched Ursula shine her smile on him, maternal, devoted. When he brought McKenzie back to her after the lesson and said, "She's really progressing, Mom," he was breathing differently—faster, shallower. His eyes were huge. He'd missed her.

Jamie took his ten-minute break and followed Ursula to the parking lot, so Evelyn clocked out for her own break and trailed after them. She didn't hide, but pretended to get something out of her car. She unlocked it, opened the door, and watched from a few cars away as Ursula buckled the toddler into her seat. By the time Ursula had closed the back door, Jamie had come up behind her and pressed her against the car, kissing her with a force that knocked her head against the window. Her belly was large and round between them, tender as a heat blister, and Jamie's hands were on her enormous breasts. He pushed her cardigan open and Evelyn could see the wet splotch on her left breast. Jamie's hand moved over the wetness and he made a sound—a moan against her mouth.

Evelyn shut her car door without thinking, and when she looked up, Jamie was gone and Ursula was getting in her car. In another moment, the SUV was driving out of the lot and Jamie was standing in front of her, breathing heavily, his face holding nothing of the tenderness earlier.

"What are you doing?" he asked. "Were you watching me?"

"Nothing. No. I didn't see—" Evelyn waved her hand back toward the spot where the car had been parked. "I didn't see nothing—anything."

She tried to move past him but he blocked her, eyes bright and shining.

"Did you follow me?"

"No—no. I haven't been—Ursula—"

Jamie's mouth twitched. "Have you been following me?"

Evelyn tried to move around him but he put a hand on her shoulder, pushing her back. She was trapped between the cars. He was close—she could feel a vulcanized heat pulsing from him.

"Don't follow me." A growl, something from the throat, resonating in the jawbone, lips parted to show teeth, straight and white with the slight overlap in the bottom incisors. She'd been told not to smile at the dog—that the dog didn't understand smiling and saw it as a threat. She was staring at Jamie's teeth, sharp and shining wet, the faint glitter of tongue, and she lunged forward and bit him in the face. He jumped back with a yelp.

They were two people staring at one another. He reached up to touch his bleeding lip.

"You bit me," he said, eyes big.

She couldn't think. She needed to think. She pushed the heels of her hands into her eye sockets to focus her vision. She licked her lips and tasted the coppery tang of Jamie's blood.

"I'm sorry. Jesus." She was waving her hands.

Jamie looked at the blood on his fingers as a string of pink saliva dripped down to his feet. He blinked unevenly and swayed forward.

Evelyn caught him and steadied him on her shoulder.

Together, they staggered back into the building, shuffling their weight awkwardly together until Jamie could sink shakily into a chair in the empty break room. Evelyn wetted a paper towel at the sink and sat in front of Jamie, wiping the blood off his chin and then folding the paper towel over to dab at his lip. She could see the small ragged tear on the inside, where her teeth had cut into the skin near his gum line. Jamie's watering eyes rolled up to the ceiling as he tried not to see the blood staining the paper towel—but he sat obediently, hands on his thighs.

They weren't speaking and Evelyn felt uneasy in the silence.

"I haven't been following you," she said. "You and Ursula—it's—I haven't . . ."

"Can we not talk about this here?" he said, looking around the break room.

"Sorry," she said as he winced away from the paper towel.

The hand on her shoulder, the bared teeth. It was because he loved her—Ursula, his pregnant lover. He was protective of their secret.

The wound was still bleeding lightly. Jamie left with a lip swollen to almost twice its size and got back into the pool with his next student, smiling and shrugging and saying something Evelyn couldn't understand when the mother asked what happened to his face. Evelyn cleaned the traps, monitored the pumps, and checked the water's PH, periodically looking at Jamie, and she found him staring back at her as she tasted his blood in her mouth.

When her shift ended, she passed the pool on her way to

the office to clock out. Jamie was in the pool, bobbing a goggled baby on a noodle, singing, "Sally the camel had . . . two humps," as his eyes followed Evelyn's legs across the room. His lip was still swollen, splotchy, and purple. His eyes met hers.

Evelyn went to the locker room to get her things, but when she opened her locker, she saw that it was empty. She'd taken her keys and phone with her when she followed Jamie out earlier. She'd set her things inside her car.

She walked to the parking lot, a floating mist clinging to her hair and eyelashes as she went to her car and spotted her keys and phone on the driver's seat. She tried the handle. Locked.

She stood there, mist blobbing onto her clothes and hair like fish eggs. She could go inside, see if anyone had a wire coat hanger that she could use to jimmy open the door—it might work. Packy had always kept a spare key in the wheel well of the undercarriage, and now she wondered why she hadn't done the same.

Evelyn stood and watched as the sun slid low across the western mountains, a sallow bleed behind the cloud cover that sharpened forest shadows. She should've been driving home. In a couple of hours, she'd be making dinner for Lila and Mora, getting them washed and in bed. Getting ready for another night shift—another slow roll of night into day, into night.

How long had she been standing there? Water was dripping from the ends of her hair. She pressed her fingers to her eyebrows and trickles of water ran down into her eyes. The lake wind rolled the cypresses and cedars, sweeping up into the wilder hills—to larches gone yellow and shedding their needles, ashy white trunks of alders gleaming in the shadows like clavicles. And a few cars away was Jamie's champagne-colored Geo. She could see the lock standing up on the sill of the driver's side window.

Evelyn went to his car and opened the door. She got in.

The car smelled like Jamie—his deodorant, his shampoo, an undercurrent of chlorine, a cloud of him. It was an old car but surprisingly clean. No fast-food wrappers or empty water bottles, no loose change on the seats. She settled her weight in the driver's seat, feeling her joints crack and the vertebrae of her spine pop. She let her hips spread and her neck loosen—painful at first, but then there was relief, a feeling of exhalation. Of rest. She closed her eyes.

Soon, she realized she was asleep but couldn't move or rouse herself. Her mouth was hanging open and she couldn't close it, trapped in a fetal paralysis. She could hear cars driving in and out of the parking lot—knew she was visible to anyone who walked past the car, but she hung suspended in a liminal sleep. Nan once told her about the cholera epidemics of the eighteenth and nineteenth centuries, about people falling into comas and appearing to be dead, being buried—and then years later, exhumed, fingernail scratches on the inside of the coffin lid.

As Evelyn sat in the car, unable to move, she dreamed of her body being carried away, presumed dead, but hearing and seeing all as she was sunk in the lake, stones in her pockets, drifting down, down, down, to the cold, black bottom to drift like a ghost, dragging her toes through the silt.

She became aware of footsteps on wet asphalt. She tried to open her eyes, sit up—but she lay pinned in place by the weight of her exhaustion, and listened as the footsteps came closer. Jamie.

And then someone was yelling—a woman. A yelp of surprise. Evelyn sat up, eyes blinking. It took her a moment to focus on the scene outside the car. A woman in an oversized University of Washington sweatshirt with the sleeves rolled up to her elbows was shouting, throwing something—at Jamie, who was standing in the middle of the parking lot, dodging whatever she hurled at him.

"—like to fuck pregnant women—" she shouted.

She was throwing boxes of condoms at him.

"Sarah!" he called. "Stop!"

Evelyn opened the door and stepped out, but neither the woman nor Jamie saw her. She crouched and duckwalked behind the next car as the woman ran out of boxes to throw and went to her SUV. The back door was open. Evelyn saw the infant car seat and the peek of tiny pink toes before the woman shut the door.

Evelyn drove home in the dark, the wind buffeting the car on the highway as the tree shadows swung. She'd only slept for two hours in Jamie's car, but it was enough and she didn't stop on the way for coffee.

When she reached the house, the lights were on and she could see Nan and Mora sitting at the table eating dinner. Mora was slapping her hands in the food on her tray as Nan speared an egg noodle with her fork and held it to Mora's mouth. Evelyn opened the door and Nan didn't look up from the quivering noodle as she said, "Out with your *bel homme?*"

Evelyn paused in the entryway, coat halfway off.

"What?" she asked.

Nan looked up now. "You need to call if you're going to be late." The noodle fell off the fork, and Rosie, lying on the floor under Mora's high chair, snapped at it. Nan didn't seem to notice that the noodle had fallen and she still held the fork out.

Evelyn hung up her coat before kneeling to unlace her boots. "Sorry. I wasn't thinking."

FAITH MERINO

She left her boots in the entryway and went to the couch, where Lila was curled up in sleep. She wasn't wheezing, but her breaths came with a popping, crackling sound.

"Why does she sound like that? When'd you last give her a treatment?" Evelyn asked.

"This morning. She's not wheezing," said Nan. "It's stridor—inflammation of the tissue in her windpipe. The nebulizer won't do anything for it, but it's nothing to worry about."

Evelyn stroked Lila's forehead and the little girl's eyes fluttered slightly, just enough to show the rolling aqueous green of an iris, and Evelyn felt the familiar crush in her ribcage. Guilt. She was never home.

When Mora was finished with dinner, Evelyn took both girls to bed and circled herself around them, still in her jeans and socks from yesterday. Mora wasn't ready to sleep and flopped around, dancing her hands in the air, walking her feet up the wall. Lila lay still, head tipped back, mouth open trustingly. She fit so neatly into Evelyn's middle. Evelyn put her nose in Lila's hair and breathed in deeply. Her scalp was musty—she hadn't been bathed in over a week.

By the time Mora fell asleep, Nan had already gone to bed and Evelyn could hear Rosie's gruff snores as she slipped out of the room in fresh jeans and a T-shirt. She crept through the quiet house to put on her jacket and boots—Nan had put them in the garage. Evelyn opened the garage door to get them off the top step, but a quiet, brushing sound made her stop. It was rhythmic. Understated. It was breathing.

She tried to focus her eyes in the dark and saw a shadow moving on the other side of the garage. She could smell the familiar sulfurous chemical odor. Erin.

She turned on the light and no one was there, but just above the workbench where the sound had come from, a mangled, headless mourning dove hung from a screw in the wall. Erin showing her that she could get inside.

The night she found Mora in the tub, Evelyn had been asked to work a double. She'd considered it but wanted to get home to check on the girls. Erin had only been home for three weeks. She'd moved the playpen into her bedroom and went back to changing diapers and making breakfast. Lila had looked at Evelyn often during those weeks, her eyes finding Evelyn's across the room when Erin said, "Come on, lovebug, it's time for bed." The first night, Lila sneaked out of Erin's room and into Evelyn's. After that, Erin latched the chain on her bedroom door at night. She corrected both girls when they called Evelyn "Mama," taking their faces in her red-knuckled hands and making them look into her lashless eyes as she said, "I'm here. I'm your mama."

On the night Evelyn came home to Mora rolling underwater in the tub, she grabbed the baby by her hair. She'd never pick up a baby like that, but she grabbed her by the hair and an arm and yanked her out of the tub. Mora had gasped and coughed, and Evelyn held her tight, the wet baby soaking the front of her shirt and jeans. She'd clutched her, feeling Mora's ribs shuddering with each cry—a mourning death wail. The baby had become something amphibious as she twisted in the tub—something in between, existing in two different dimensions. She'd punctured the membrane, had swung out with the stars, the disorder of planets and suns, the violent dazzle of galaxies, and she'd seen where her universe ended. She was crying because there had been no one there. She'd been alone.

Now Evelyn had nightmares. She sometimes dreamed she was the baby, sitting in the tub, staring down at the swirling, pink grease patina on the water, then slipping under, unable to pull herself up, belching big bubbles of air.

Sometimes she dreamed she was Lila, watching the baby flounder and twist, going out to get help and trying to speak but finding no words, just croaking out bubbles.

Sometimes she dreamed she got home one minute later.

Now she dreamed she was Erin walking up the porch steps to Nan's house. She was letting herself in. She'd come to take everything Evelyn had—to take back what had been stolen from her.

She hadn't planned to go back to Jamie's car, but the promise of sleep was too powerful to give up, and when she went out to the parking lot after her shift and spotted his car, she walked right past her own.

Jamie's car was warm and musky smelling, and the windshield was already beginning to fog with her warmth. She lowered the driver's seat down and set her alarm for one hour—his shift would be over in two.

She fell asleep to the sound of the wind whistling through the slightly cracked back window, so rhythmic and lulling that when her alarm went off an hour later, she couldn't open her eyes to turn it off. She was aware of the loud beeping, of the danger of being caught, but she couldn't move, hanging in the same deathlike sleep as before, drifting along the bottom of the lake—feet falling away, then hands, arms, head, until she was little more than a backbone sliding through the sediment in the shredded swirling remnants of her clothes.

The alarm might have been going off for two or three hours when she felt the blast of cold air and a hard, heavy hand on her shoulder. Jamie was talking, voice harsh, but Evelyn still couldn't rouse herself. When he began shaking her, she opened her eyes but couldn't focus.

"What are you doing in my car?" he was saying.

She winced and moved heavily as she stepped into the stinging chill, the wind whipping her hair in her mouth and eyes.

"Are you okay?" Jamie asked, putting a hand on her elbow. His voice sounded underwater.

He was looking around the parking lot for her car. He started to close his door but stopped, went rigidly still, staring at the seat, and she saw what he was looking at: a near-perfect circle of red blood. His mouth was open slightly and she could see the wet, pink glisten of tongue—just a quick flash, a catch of the light.

She left him there and went back to her car. It was already dark when she got on the highway and drove south, stopping at the Foxy Lady on the way home. She was light-headed, and her vision flickered like old fluorescents as she ordered a coffee at the counter, and then pushed through the blue cloud of cigarette smoke to the bathrooms. In the stall, she pulled down her pants and saw the blood in her underwear, the blood that had seeped through her jeans to leave a dark stain.

The following Monday, Jamie came to work while Evelyn was cleaning out the traps. She watched as he disappeared into the employee break room to hang up his gym bag in his locker before getting in the pool. It wasn't until he was swimming with his first student—a skinny five-year-old boy in oversized trunks—that he flashed his eyes up at her as he said, "All right, Houston, what flavors are we scooping today? Let's get those scoopers out." He kept his eyes on her as he guided the boy across the pool, singing, "Ice cream, ice cream, chocolate and vanilla . . ."

The edge of fear in his eyes from the previous week was gone. Now he was watching her with glimmering curiosity. When she crossed the room to take her break, his eyes tracked her.

He hadn't cleaned the blood off the seat. She saw it when she peeked through the passenger window as she walked through the parking lot. The stain was still there, now a cloudy, rust-red blot that he was sitting on every time he got in the car, that he saw every time he opened the door. She could feel her heartbeat in her fingertips: fear, embarrassment, but also a feeling of expansion.

But she couldn't leave it, so she went back inside the building, into the pump room to fill a bucket halfway with soapy water. She carried it out to the parking lot with a scrub brush and opened the driver's side door.

"Don't," Jamie said behind her, making her jump.

She steadied herself and turned to face him. He was in his swim shirt and trunks, with a towel around his waist, hair falling ragged and wet around his face. He had to be freezing. The sun had come out—it was an unusually clear day, sunlight angled sideways and blazing upward from the puddles on the asphalt—but the cold breeze was slicing.

Evelyn cleared her throat. "I gotta clean it."

"Why?" He looked at her levelly, unblinking—not a challenging stare.

Evelyn swallowed, throat dry and gritty. "Because it's . . . dirty."

He shook his head. "No," he said. "I like it."

Evelyn looked away and Jamie didn't say anything more. When she looked at him again, his eyes were gas-flame-blue rings, and they didn't leave her face.

Evelyn stared at him, at the shifting shadow under his clavicle, at the twitch of muscle in his jaw, at the quick grip of the tendons in his neck. His body was all movement.

"Why do you like pregnant women?" she asked.

Jamie sighed through his nose. He didn't seem surprised by the question.

"Because," he said patiently, "I like the way they look."

"Why?"

"I don't know. Why do you sleep in my car?"

"Because it's the only place I can sleep."

"Why?"

Evelyn shrugged. "I don't know."

They both fell silent. Jamie was watching her face, his jaw set, mouth tight. He chewed the inside of his cheek for a moment before saying, "I don't know why I like them. I just do—I always have."

"Are any of them yours? The babies?" Evelyn asked.

Jamie shook his head thoughtfully. "No." She couldn't tell if his tone was disappointed or neutral.

They both went quiet again.

"But sometimes I pretend they are. Sometimes I pretend that I've gotten her pregnant, and then that makes me come right there on the spot."

Something about it made her slick-slippery. Pregnant. Broken open, membrane breached, seeded. When Evelyn found her breath, she straightened herself. They'd been outside too long. They'd gone well over their ten minutes.

"Tanya's gonna write you up," said Evelyn, gesturing with the scrub brush to the main entrance.

She knelt and dunked the scrub brush in the soapy water, but Jamie grabbed her hand, making her drop the brush.

"No." He was looking at her face as he said, "It's *my* car."

"It's *my* blood," Evelyn said, yanking her hand away.

Jamie set his jaw.

"Jamie!" Tanya yelled from the door. "What the hell are you doing? Joey Munson is waiting for his lesson. He's moving up to Piranha today!"

"Coming," Jamie said, grabbing the bucket of water before heading inside.

Evelyn stayed by the car for a moment, crouched at eye level with her own blood. She stood up and shut the door, following Jamie in to finish her shift. His eyes found her as she moved around the aquatic center, but they didn't speak again. After she clocked out, she drove home, stopping for coffee, knowing that she wouldn't be sleeping before her night shift, wondering if Jamie would look for her in the parking lot. Would he see her blood on his seat and miss her? Would he think about her while he was having sex with a mother leaking milk from her breasts, her taut water-globe belly pressed between them?

When she pulled up to the house, she saw movement in the front window—Nan picking up Mora, carrying her to the bedroom—and Evelyn got out of her car. As she walked up the marshy yellow lawn, a car came down the road. It drove slowly past the house, and she saw the round, white jawbone in the passenger's-side window, the wheat-red hair, and lashless eyes.

She blinked, and the passenger's seat was empty. In another moment, the car was gone.

NAN

The December cold came sharp and fast—a predator striking out—and suddenly there was snow, blankets of it falling on cedars and spruces like someone had upended a sack of flour. It piled up in drifts that would eventually harden and crust over but for now were playful and light. And there was the quiet—the silence that came with the snowfall.

When Lila wheezed and rattled, Nan wrapped her in blankets and took her outside to the clean, cold air, alone in a circle of trees. The snow gathered on the pine branches. Slowly, Lila's breathing would come clear again.

That was where Nan saw Clara coming one morning, a flicker of movement between the bony aspens. She was hazy in the distance but became sharper, more defined as she got closer, edging carefully around the wet sword ferns—always in her thin yellow cardigan, despite the freezing air.

"You know what'll make her better," Clara called.

"Shh," Nan hissed, pointing a finger at Lila, who slept on her shoulder, flakes of snow catching in her hair. One snagged in her eyelashes and Nan picked it out with trembling fingers.

Clara came around the gnarled, mossy trunk of an old maple. She touched the wet moss and winced, stopping to wipe her wet hand on her skirt.

"I don't know why you're letting that girl suffer," said Clara.

"The nebulizer is helping," said Nan. "The antibiotics just need time to kick in."

"Rain is coming. If you don't get out there soon, ice'll kill everything."

The snow had already blanketed the ground in a thick layer of powder and Nan could feel it soaking into her shoes, the cold settling into the bones of her feet. She realized Lila's bare toes were hanging out of the blankets and she pulled the quilts tighter around the girl, feeling a sudden, clutching swell of love—a desperate need to protect her. The same desperate protectiveness Evelyn likely felt when she made an animal den of herself around the little girls in bed every night.

Nan carried Lila inside, leaving Clara out in the cold, but knowing she was right.

Not waiting for the snowfall to lighten, she put on her jacket, zipped the little girls into their parkas, and carried them out to the freezing car. Rosie let herself out and followed them, hopping into the front seat and sitting upright, alert. Nan drove slowly down the steep hill, tires crunching through snow as she turned onto Linden Lane and parked at the chained gate. She left the car running so the heater would keep the girls warm as she got out, Rosie following, and edged around the glazed gate posts. She trudged up the road, Rosie trotting close behind, but in another moment, the dog had caught a scent and disappeared.

The road, once carefully cultivated with rosebushes and elders, was now overgrown with ferns and weeds. When she came to the rise in the road, she looked back at the idling car, stewing in a cloud of exhaust that had nowhere to go in the cold. Lila had fallen asleep, twisted around in her seat so that her face was buried in the headrest, but Mora was awake and Nan could see her feathery red curls as she turned her head one way and the other.

Nan kept walking, leaving them behind as she trudged up the steep incline that made her knees ache. She hadn't dressed for the weather. Her tennis shoes slipped in the frozen mud and she fell on her knees twice, staining her blue jeans. On the other side of the rise, the road dipped just as sharply and she slipped and hit the ground. She could feel the ice wetting through her underwear as she stood up and headed down to the low point in the road, which had flooded, as it always did this time of year, leaving a silvery lake that was as pure and clear as a window. She scanned the water until she found the curb on the side of the road and edged along it, feet still sliding into a few inches of water that soaked her socks. Someone watching from a distance would see her walking on water.

She hadn't gone this far in years—decades—and somewhere, she could hear Clara moving through the pine boughs and cracking through the bracken.

"Come on, they're still there," Clara called to her. Nan followed her voice—a watery echo farther up the road.

She used to be able to smell the rhododendrons before she rounded the bend—heavy-headed flowers that loomed in huge, red blood bursts—walls of them in front of the house. But now the hedges were snowed over, leaving no trace of the blooms, and Nan's gut clutched at the memory of the house. The Tooley mansion had been left to rot and the roof had collapsed in spots. Teenagers in town talked about Friday night challenges to go into the house alone. They talked about the sweeping main staircase covered in a thick, hard crust of bird shit from roosting owls and blackbirds. The smell of musty feathers and rat nests. They talked about trying to climb the stairs to the second floor, feeling the give of soft, rotting wood beneath their feet, the pants-shitting fear that a sole would split the film of the old carpet and the whole staircase could collapse, vacuuming the climber into a dark, unknowable black.

When Nan came around the overgrown elders, she saw the house as clearly as she had all those years ago: towering and church-like in its steepled height perched at the top of the hill. The octagonal tower rose out of the pine trees like a giant claw—the only part of the house that was visible from the town below, where people could see the slate shingles gathering snow in the winter, moss in the spring. The whole thing was laced with ivy that leafed in the winter.

And was that the rabbling, rumbling crowd gathered around the house? People from the town, people from other towns, people from other states—all waiting to see the Boy Without a Face? They were all waiting to pay a dollar to see Peter. There was a neatly painted sign staked in the ground in front of the porch: $1/viewing.

Nan stood still, breath hanging in a hot fog around her face as she stared up at the house, at the people below, at the sign—an arrow pointing left, toward the greenhouse, where the boy was playing, and the surgeon's housekeeper would usher in viewers one at a time to see him.

"Come on. Don't get stuck," said Clara. "Keep moving."

Nan stepped closer and saw the greenhouse as it was then: glass panes lit silver by the sky, dripping with condensation from the muggy heat inside, flowers growing huge and flushed with life. She knew without seeing him that Peter was in there, running through the rows of plants, laughing and feeling with his hands.

"What are you doing?" Nan called out.

Clara was halfway through the greenhouse door and she looked back at Nan, eyebrows raised in languid surprise.

"You wanna get them plants, don't you? Well, here's where they're at," she said, pointing to the back of the greenhouse. That was where the surgeon kept his medicinal plants—poppies, coca plants, but also marshmallow plants. Soaked in water, the marshmallow roots became gelatinous, released their mucilage. Strained and sipped, they loosened tight coughs.

"After all these years? All this time?" Nan said.

Clara stopped and looked at her in blunt disbelief now. "You come all this way and *now* you're gonna doubt it? Go see for yourself."

"Is he in there?" Nan asked.

"He ain't in there," Clara said. "I told you. Where he is now, he don't hear me when I call him."

Nan flinched, reminded again—as she always was, as she always would be—that she was responsible.

"I ain't here to try to make you apologize again. I'm too tired for all that. Just come on and get the girl's medicine," said Clara.

Nan twisted the collar of her shirt between her fingers. She adjusted her bra and rolled her shoulders, and then approached the door, but as she got closer, the greenhouse changed. The silver-lit glass browned, turned scummy and cloudy until she couldn't see the flowers inside anymore. The iron frame turned to rust as she neared it, an optical illusion—a change of light—and when she finally reached the door that had rotted off its hinges, she could see that the inside was nothing more than a dried tangle of brambles and vines. She looked at Clara, but Clara was gone.

She didn't go inside. She moved around the north wall to where the marshmallow plants were—tall green stalks shelved with pointed, downy leaves. In the summer, pink starbursts bloomed at the leaf axils. Nan moved closer and rubbed one furred leaf between thumb and forefinger, remembering the surgeon's smooth hands and rounded fingertips doing the same before reaching down and scooping into the loam, digging out the spidery roots of one of the stalks. As he dug, he told her, "These plants aren't native to North America, but they do well in this climate. They adapt." He turned his face up to her, his pale eyes glinting silver under the white sky, like the windows behind him. "Marshmallow is one of the miracles of nature, but we scientists are too much in our own way to see it."

"Do you believe in miracles?" Nan asked.

Doctor Linden looked at the root in his hands and brushed it absently as he stood up. He hadn't lived on the south shore for very long. His third winter. He was wearing a cotton cable-knit sweater because he hadn't yet learned to stick to wool, which kept the snow from soaking through to the skin. She'd noticed that he didn't shave on the weekends and his jaw was stippled with a day's growth of black beard, which gave their meeting a strange sense of intimacy. She'd come for the plants. She'd come for him.

Linden went to the potting bench and set the marshmallow plants down to cut off the stems and wrap the roots in burlap. "I believe in species as a state of becoming, that all species are in a constant state of flux as life adapts and evolves. I believe in genetic mutations—the kind that come along once in a millennia, like Peter—that allow a species to adapt, become something better than itself. Those mutations sometimes appear monstrous." He looked back at Peter, who sat quietly on Nan's hip—she was caring for him while Clara worked at the logging camp. "But I believe we're all monsters."

And Peter, before he was known as the Boy Without a Face, sat listening—she could tell by the forward tilt of his head—listening to the currents and frequencies that sang over his head. Did he recognize the voice of the surgeon who had opened his hip, chipped off flakes of bone, and grafted them into the hole in the roof of his mouth when he was five months old? Did he know the voice of the man who had crushed the bone above his nose to realign it, sutured his gaping eye sockets partially closed, and loosened the twists of skin connecting the corners of his mouth to his lower eyelids in a grisly, court-jester grin?

Nan had been with Clara when the nurses brought her to him after the surgery—a piteous thing splayed out on the table, sedated, bandages pocked with dark blood. And Clara's liquid center had swung her forward so that Nan had to catch her, and Nan stayed there with them as Clara held Peter all night long and spoke her love not in words, but in hums, sighs, and moans.

A year after the surgery, Peter's weight felt easy, natural on Nan's hip. He tensed and then coughed a tight, barking cough.

Linden handed her the wrapped root as he said, "Chop up one inch of this and soak it in a glass of water for a few hours. Put a little sugar in it to get him to drink it and the cough will be gone in a day or two."

Nan looked at the surgeon's face, at his pale eyes as they flashed on hers. She felt her own baby jump in the moonrise of her belly—a baby girl that would be born dead in a few weeks. Nan took the muddy root from him and his fingers brushed hers, cold and gritty with earth.

At home, Nan chopped up an inch of marshmallow root and soaked it in a glass of water. She left the rest to dry, spread thin on a paper towel under a lamp. When the tea was ready, she stirred in some sugar, poured the mixture in a sippy cup, and took it to Lila, who was awake on the couch, Rosie curled in sleep beside her. When Nan sat down beside her, Lila said, "I hungry."

"Drink some juice first," said Nan, bringing the sippy cup to Lila's lips.

Lila was awake more these days as the nebulizer opened her airways. She was still sluggish and her breathing still rankled in her chest, but her lips were no longer blue.

As Lila finished off the last of the tea, the door opened and Evelyn came in with a sweep of cold wind and a pizza box in one hand. It was three o'clock, there was still daylight outside.

Evelyn smiled at Lila and said, "Look who's up."

Mora backslid off the coffee table and charged across the room to Evelyn with arms out.

"You're home early," said Nan.

Evelyn set the pizza on the table and carried Mora to the couch to sit beside Lila, kissing her on the head.

"Not really," she said, smiling at Mora and blowing raspberries on her neck so that the baby tipped her head back with a gallop of laughter. Lila was looking up at her—still pale and glassy-eyed, head jutting forward on her skinny neck, but with a new, steady focus Evelyn hadn't seen in weeks.

Evelyn carried Mora into the kitchen and put her in the high chair before opening the pantry and getting the paper plates off the high shelf.

"Don't waste the paper plates on this," said Nan, bringing Lila to the table.

"I'm not wasting them if I'm using them to put food on," Evelyn said as she set out napkins and a plastic fork and knife for Nan.

She opened the box and released a cloud of sulfurous garlic, tomato sauce, and sweet dough. As she lifted the slices and set them on plates, Nan sat down at her seat. She was picky about ingredients. She could smell the chemical agents that made the sauce brighter, that kept the cheese from sticking to itself, that kept the dough from growing mold. It made her throat tighten with nausea. Evelyn was looking at her wearily, her dark hair tucked behind her ears so that Nan could see the tinselly glitter of gray at her temples.

Nan helped Mora eat to avoid sitting idle and drawing attention to her own refusal to eat the stuff. But Evelyn noticed and gestured at the pie with the slice in her own hand.

"Are you really not gonna eat it?" she asked.

"You know I don't like pizza."

Evelyn didn't say anything as her eyes fixed on something behind Nan, out the front window. Nan turned around and spotted Jubilee and Paulie Grimmley coming up the porch steps. Jube stopped at the window and peered in, knocked on the glass, and waved to them. Then, a knock at the door. Evelyn's large, black eyes met Nan's, waiting to be told what to do. Nan went to the door, opened it just wide enough to see out, but Jube already had her hand on the door and was pushing it open.

"I *heard* there were two of them," she called into the house. "I had to hear it through Linney Bradford."

She was already in the house as Nan stepped back and said, "Come in."

Paulie followed her inside, too tall, stooped, still moving through the world with the same bowl cut and thick beard that had swallowed up his narrow face since the 1980s. He glanced at Nan and nodded once.

Jube went to the table and bent down to look at Mora, wrinkling her nose to make a face. Mora stared with big eyes. "Do you know who I am?" Jube asked in a loud, clear voice, as though speaking to someone with hearing loss. She looked at Lila. "I'm your grandma."

"We were just going," said Evelyn, looking at the floor as she scooted away from the table and stood up.

"Well, don't let me chase you out. I just wanted to come see my grandbabies for myself." As if to demonstrate, she bent over Mora again and scrutinized the baby's wide-eyed face. "They must take after their father. They don't look a thing like you. You definitely got your daddy's coloring—pure Indian. You could almost pass for purebred."

Evelyn was hugging her elbows, looking at the floor.

"Can you say, *Grandma*?" Jube said to Mora.

Mora stared back at her blankly, and Jube laughed, which looked more like a grimace.

Nan watched, knowing that Jube wouldn't touch the girls. She'd never been one for touching. She'd been a timid girl growing up. Never sitting next to other girls in school, flinching from loud noises—she once ran crying to the bathroom, startled, when a cart full of plastic trays tipped over in the cafeteria and sent metal dishes clanking and clattering to the floor. Nan had been Jube's science teacher in the ninth grade. She once touched her on the shoulder in passing and was startled herself as both of Jube's arms flew out, like a spider rearing from a wasp.

"We really were just leaving—Lila's been sick. I was about to take her to the doctor," said Evelyn, grabbing the girls' puffy, blue yard sale parkas and stocking caps off the coat rack.

Jube didn't say anything as Evelyn squatted down to zip up Lila and pull the stocking cap over her head—too big, so that it slipped down over her eyes. All that could be seen was Lila's nose and wispy tufts of hair. Evelyn looked up at Nan, her eyes full of meaning, and Nan zipped Mora's parka and grabbed her purse to follow Evelyn out. But as Evelyn walked to the door,

Jube said forcefully, "I'm making your Grandpa Royce's special ham for Christmas. You remember his secret ingredient: the cheapest spiral cut on sale." She laughed arrhythmically.

"Help yourselves to some pizza," said Nan, snapping her fingers at Rosie, who jumped up and followed her out the door.

Jube and Paulie were still standing by the dining room table as Nan backed the Crown Victoria out of the gravel driveway.

They drove down the mud road, made a circle around the town, and by the time they came home half an hour later, it was raining and Jube and Paulie were gone.

The next day, Nan watched Evelyn as she moved with brisk, purposeful strides through the house, got old sheets out of the linen closet and carried them outside to pack around the pipes. The freezing rain hadn't stopped since the previous night.

Evelyn had already shut off the water. She'd opened all the taps and faucets. She went out to the garage and filled buckets with the water left in the water heater. She lugged each one—ten in all—to the back porch so the girls wouldn't fall in them and get stuck. Nan watched her, blanched white under the gray gasp of sky, as she lined the buckets against the wall of the house and then covered each one with a plastic lid to keep debris out.

They'd already filled the pots and pitchers and serving bowls with water. Before Evelyn shut the water off, Nan had suggested they fill up the bathtub, but Evelyn barked, "No," in a loud, abrupt voice that made Nan jump. Evelyn shook her head, hands flapping awkwardly as if not knowing what to do with them before she rubbed her eyes and said, "It's—" She shook her head again before finishing. "It wouldn't make a difference. We'd have to heat the water to wash up anyway," she said. And then she walked past Nan to tuck sheets in the gap under the door.

By midmorning, ice was slicking the porch steps and the mud road outside. The wire fence that divided Nan's property from that of Jim Sandoval was swinging in a two-inch-thick cylinder of ice.

Now, Evelyn was splitting wood in her thick ski jacket with the ripped seam, tufts of fluff sticking out. Raising her arms over her head, her back opened and she brought the ax down on the wood so that the trees echoed with the cracking of the logs. She was twiny, but she could make herself big when she had to.

The wood was wet and Evelyn piled it on the back porch to keep it out of the rain, saving it for when they really needed it.

After dinner, the power went out, leaving them in darkened silence.

Evelyn built a fire, constructing a scaffolding of kindling in the woodstove and topping it with a large, wet, green log that would produce a cloud of smoke.

"We gotta watch Mora around the woodstove," she said, standing up and wiping her hands on her jeans. In another moment, she was gone, reappearing minutes later dragging the queen mattress from her bedroom.

It didn't take long for the cold to settle in, creeping along the floor and exhaling from the corners of the house. Rosie lay asleep on the rug, but sat up suddenly, sniffed at her own crotch, and moved to another spot on the rug because she'd been refusing to go out in the cold to pee and was now leaking in her sleep.

The last time Cormorant Lake had an ice storm was in 1961.

"Remind me to caulk the windows after this," Evelyn said as she fed another green log to the fire. Smoke muscled out of the stove door and crawled up the wall. She was kneeling, one elbow on her raised knee and her back rounding like a beetle shell, and Nan saw Margaret kneeling in the snow, over the frozen fish skeleton—saw Margaret look up at her and say, "Will you take her?"

That night, they all slept on two mattresses pushed together in front of the woodstove. Nan was used to going to bed at eight thirty every night, but now she lay awake in a half doze, Mora's head tucked into her armpit, breath hanging in the air since the fire's warmth only reached so far, even with the door of the woodstove open. Sometimes Nan closed her eyes and opened them and Evelyn was asleep in the other bed, wrapped up with Lila. Then she closed her eyes and opened them to find Evelyn squatting by the fire, stoking it, feeding more logs to the sinewy flames. Evelyn was afraid the girls would get up and touch the stove, so she didn't sleep for more than a few minutes at a time. When Nan closed and opened her eyes again, Evelyn was back in bed and Clara was sitting on a stool by the closed door of the stove, staring at the orange, glowing window.

"What did she mean by that?" Nan asked, rising up on her elbow. "'Will you take her?' What did she mean by that? Did she mean would I take care of Jube after she left? Or did she mean would I take her away from her parents?"

Clara shrugged. "Hell if I know. Probably both."

"Why would she say that?"

Clara gave Nan a meaningful stare. "Why do you think?"

Nan went quiet. Her role in the tragedy of Peter Lark was well known. No husband, no money, and more surgeries in Peter's future, Clara had had to take a job as a cook's assistant in the Tooley logging camp, a day's train ride away, and she couldn't bring Peter with her, so she left him with Nan. Eight months later, she came home to the signs at the train station, on the highways, posted on drugstore doors: Come See the Boy

Without a Face. Everyone knew that was Nan's doing. Nan had given Peter away.

"It wasn't my fault, though . . ." Nan whispered. "It was. Of course it was. Clara, I didn't know he was going to keep him. He tricked me."

Clara's lips pressed together crookedly and she looked back into the flames.

"It don't matter. All of that's done." She said, "Sleep now."

And like a spell, Nan closed her eyes. When she awoke, it was morning and Evelyn was crouched at the open door of the woodstove, wrapped in the lace-trimmed, floral bedspread. Nan sat up and Evelyn looked at her.

"Are you okay?" Evelyn asked, wiping her wet, pink nose with her wrist. "You were talking in your sleep last night."

Nan waved her off. "I'm fine, just old." And she got up to make the coffee. The air was gasping cold and hit her like a slap of water when she came out from under the blankets. She snatched the afghan off the couch and swung it around herself as Evelyn smiled.

"Go look outside," Evelyn said, nodding at the window.

Nan went to the window and saw the glittering winter world outside, everything encased in ice—the car, the porch, hung with leaning icicles where the wind had blown the rain slantways. Across the road at the house Jube grew up in, the tarps perpetually wadded in the yard and pooled with brown water were now frozen solid and sparkling with frost, as were the scattered camper shells and lawn mower parts. Every blade of grass, every pine bough and needle—all were shimmering laceworks of ice. The trees drooped heavily under the weight—one had fallen onto the power lines, which, themselves, were glistening beams.

While Nan stared breathlessly out the window, Evelyn was already moving swiftly across the house, dragging in four buckets of frozen water from outside and setting them near the fire to thaw. In the kitchen, she ladled water from a serving bowl into a pot, floating a rubber banded filter of coffee grounds. She lit the gas burner with a match.

Nan made breakfast in the same way while Mora and Lila sat on the mattresses, cocooned in blankets and breathing slowly, their breaths puffing out as clouds. Rosie lay under the blankets with them, refusing to emerge even to eat from the bowl Nan had placed by the stove. Nan balanced a bowl in her lap as she sat on the mattress to spoon-feed the girls one bite at a time—and as she brought the spoon to Mora's open mouth, she remembered doing the same thing in the last ice storm. Peter was wrapped in a blanket and she was bringing the spoon to his open mouth, touching it to his lower lip to show him where it was, metal clinking his tiny little teeth that glittered in the firelight. The air was dry from the woodstove, and she used a small, damp handkerchief to gently wipe the red of his turned-out eyelids, the way Clara had shown her, so that they wouldn't get irritated.

He laughed as he ran through the house. He knew where he was going because he had the layout memorized—his house, the house Clara had grown up in—and he ran through it until he was pink-cheeked and sweaty despite the cold, never once hitting a table corner or chair. Nan knew she should tell him not to run in the house, but she couldn't dampen his joy—it would be cruel.

The ice storm froze the hinges and iced the doorknobs, and she, Peter, and the jumping baby in her belly were huddled together in Clara's house. Peter pressed his whole body to Nan's in the night, and she woke up with his face nuzzling her arm, and she thought she couldn't get any happier, even with Earl gone. Earl, with his big eyes and shy, crooked smile, who'd written long, smudged letters to her while she was in college and he was working in the Tooley Timber Company logging camp—who told her how the winter cold cracked the men's mustaches off, how snow got in their boots and made their feet swampy, so they had to slice open the soles for drainage, who wrote of felling trees as big as houses, and the screaming sound they made as they crashed through the canopy, concussing in his bones when they hit the ground.

Earl, who wrote of the fires that blazed across the mountains and the film of soot that covered everything, of how the company moved on and left behind blackened earth and smoking tree stumps like a bombed city.

Earl, who stopped writing to her in her senior year, and when she came home she saw his badly burned right hand, the fingers that had curled shut, the skin too taut to open them. After their marriage, he told her of the fire that had spread in the night—of the cabins that went up in flames as the creosote turned them into tinderboxes before the men could get out. Earl told her of the eight men who were burned alive in their bunks. He became quiet, always listening to something, whispering in his sleep. He didn't respond when she said his name.

Earl, who looked at her with eyes as still as vernal pools, so clear that she could see right down to their cold-water depths where the dark fish swam, when—five months pregnant—she asked him if he was okay.

Earl left soon after to live in Port Angeles, leaving Nan with a fast-rising belly and a mortgage she couldn't pay. Clara took her in and Earl promised to visit the new baby, but soon left Port Angeles for Victoria, and then Vancouver, and up and up until he disappeared into the arctic mist of the Yukon territory.

On the fourth day of the freeze, Evelyn climbed into the attic and came down with Nan's old plastic tree and moldy boxes of decorations.

She was restless, itchy to get out. Normally Evelyn bloomed when the girls needed her. When there were things to do and Mora needed breakfast and Lila was singing on the toilet and yelling, "Mama! I'm all done!"—Evelyn came alive like a watered plant.

But she'd never been one to stay inside for very long. She'd grown up on her front porch and now that she was shut indoors with little hands grabbing at her at all hours, she was flinching and snatching herself away, sucking in her breath sharply. Nan tried to keep the girls out of the way while Evelyn put the tree together and hung tinsel garlands around the house.

"I spy with my little eye . . ." Lila called to Evelyn. "Something that's Mama's coat, and it's right there." Pointing at Evelyn's coat hanging by the door.

Evelyn knew Lila was waiting for a response, so she said wearily, "Is it my coat?" She didn't smile when Lila clapped her hands.

Evelyn got the tree up and decorated, and within hours, Mora was sitting on the mattresses, yanking the beaded garlands off the tree and looping them around Rosie's neck.

Everything smelled dusty and when Lila or Mora touched the old nativity scene, Evelyn scowled, grabbed them up, and carried them into the kitchen to wash their hands at the sink.

So on Sunday morning, despite her cracking knees and the slow twist of pain in her spine, Nan layered Lila and Mora in two pairs of pants each, two shirts, and the puffy parkas that swallowed their faces, and got the old sled out of the garage. The girls' eyes were huge and wondering as she tugged them down the crunching crystalline lawn. She walked carefully down the sloping mud road, now glazed with ice and so slick that she had to crunch her boots through the crust to make sure she gained purchase. The wind shivered through the trees, and the boughs with their ice-glass needles rolled like wind chimes, and Nan looked back at the sled, at Peter, listening, opening his mouth and tasting the bitter bite of cold air. She crunched through the ice but slipped anyway and fell with a "Whoop!" that made Peter laugh, head back, all pink tongue and hot breath and raw red nostrils.

The cold was seeping through her pants and she stood up, wiping the frozen mud off her rear as she looked back and smiled admonishingly at Lila and Mora, whose popping shrieks of laughter disappeared in the wind.

She pulled the sled down the road and turned onto Main Street, where teenagers were smoking in parking lots and sliding in their boots across frosted benches and sidewalks.

"Nan, you got a dirty butt," called Lila, and Mora fell backward laughing.

It was Sunday. The priest celebrated Mass come rain or sleet or snow.

It was Friday. Grocery day.

The new church was on Main and Third, on a gentle swell that looked out over the wooded valley to the lake beyond the pines, and Nan pulled the sled with the two little girls carefully up the hill.

The grocery store was small and the shelves were bare—the people in town had already bought up all the tinned meat and powdered milk. Nan put Peter in a shopping cart and pushed it through the empty aisles, placing a loaf of white bread in Peter's lap. She picked up a box of cake mix but put it back when she remembered that her oven wouldn't work. She found one last tin of sausages, some tomatoes, and a jar of pickled green beans.

She pulled the sled into the narthex of the church. The pews were bare, but the organist had taken her place and was playing. A scattered handful of other people had come—old women, like herself, mostly. She bent down to lift Mora out of the sled and fell.

She bent to lift Peter out of the shopping cart and fell. A tightening—a ligamentous twisting. A sky-inverting wave of force. An expulsion. Her baby.

EVELYN

Evelyn was chopping firewood out back and didn't even know Nan was gone until Ida Greene came around the side yard in her husband's thick, oversized wool jacket and her orange safety vest buckled over it, because even in this weather, she took her daily walk.

"Fell? Where?" Evelyn asked, dropping the ax.

"At the church. I was walking by it and Mary Harding told me to get you."

Ida walked with Evelyn to the church, holding a can of iodized salt that she poured on the ground ahead of them when they got onto the paved street.

The church was mostly empty except for a handful of women huddled around Nan, who sat on a chair in the narthex and stared at Evelyn with contained anger.

"We should really call you an ambulance, Nancy," said Mary Harding.

"And I told you, Mary, that I don't need a damn ambulance," said Nan, standing up and pushing away Mary's hands.

"We found her on the ground, talking to herself," Mary

said to Evelyn, ignoring Nan's scowl. "She was out of it and mumbling something about 'blood everywhere.' She needs to see a doctor."

"I'm fine. Go find someone else's business to meddle in," Nan said, walking stiffly past the women to take Evelyn's arm.

They walked home slowly, Evelyn pulling the girls in the sled and keeping her arm linked with Nan's to steady her. Nan's grip was tight as she held onto Evelyn's arm with both hands, firm and certain but with a slight tremor somewhere deep inside, and Evelyn knew as they walked together through the frozen, blue cradle of the valley—the only two people on the street—that Nan wouldn't remember why she'd gone out.

At every dip and swell in the road, at every ice slick that made Nan wobble briefly on her feet, Evelyn looked at her face to see how she was doing and saw Nan staring at the ground as if looking through it.

There was a loud, echoing crack—a low rumble, the groan of shifting bedrock, of continental unrest.

When they got home, Evelyn saw the tear in Nan's pants, just below her left knee—saw dark blood staining the fabric. When Evelyn sat Nan down on the couch and pulled her pant leg up, she found a deep cut on her shin, the purple beginnings of a bruise radiating up the bone. Evelyn made a butterfly bandage out of duct tape and taped the skin together while Nan held the girls on the couch.

"Nan got her leg hurt," Lila told Mora gravely, and Mora, eyes wide, repeated quietly, "Nan leg," which came out as "Nan yeg."

"Are you going to be okay?" Evelyn asked.

Nan waved her away. "I'll be fine."

Evelyn carried the girls into the bedroom to change them out of their wet clothes. She was tugging off Mora's pants when piano music came drifting into the room, gentle and methodical, orderly. Chopin. Evelyn listened, remembering the times she and the other children ran up the mountain road past Nan's house, from which a lonely current of piano music coursed because she was all alone inside. Sometimes Evelyn could see Nan through the lace curtains, could see her watching the children running, and she would start playing a fast, galloping song that matched their hurtling hearts as they ran into the woods.

There was something different about the song this time—missed notes, skipped beats. Nan was playing it wrong.

It was Tuesday when the ice finally thawed enough to drive the roads. Evelyn used an old credit card to scrape the frost off her windshield and then drove carefully through town, rolling in neutral since it was still too dark to see any patches of black ice. She got on the highway and headed north, toward the snowy, sun-tipped mountains as dawn broke, dreamy pink, above the pine-forest spires, feeling her lungs open and inflate at the big sky and road ahead. Being in the house the last week had felt like being trapped under a pile of rocks that were slowly compressing her ribcage, and now she rolled her window down so the arctic wind blasted her.

She got to the country club and unlocked the aquatic center doors, locking them again behind her. She turned on the heater, checked the chlorine levels, checked the traps. Tanya arrived at eight but didn't say hello. The first swim instructors showed up at eight thirty, but by nine o'clock, Jamie hadn't arrived.

When Jamie still hadn't gotten to work at ten, Evelyn ducked into the break room to check the schedule. He wasn't on it. She didn't normally make conversation with the other instructors, but as she set out the plastic chairs near a younger instructor named Kelsey, she cleared her throat awkwardly and asked, "Where's Jamie?"

Kelsey, a wide-smiling freshman at the local Christian college who was getting married next summer, guided a fat baby through the water and dunked it before saying, "He got fired." The baby came back up with a gasp and an expulsive scream. "Dating the clients," Kelsey added.

Evelyn's ribcage collapsed. She set out the last chair and walked away, hearing Kelsey mumble, "Good talk," behind her.

The rest of the day passed in atonal flatness as Evelyn finished her shift and clocked out.

Still, she showed up for work the next day with the glimmering hope she might see him—that he might be there, even though she knew better.

Each day, she finished up her shift and walked out to her car, scanning the parking lot for his, but he didn't come back. McKenzie's lessons had been discontinued and Evelyn didn't see her or her mother at the club again.

By Friday, she no longer looked for his car in the parking lot.

She finished her shift and clocked out. She got in her car and drove down the snowy mountain road, through the blue mist that made looming black bell towers of the trees, down to the main road, and west toward the lake to skirt the shoreline on her usual route home. Through the mist, she could see the vast openness beyond the trees, the ridge dropping off to a flat expanse of gray, the puckering silver of the lake. As she drove past a cove that was crowded with snowy pines, she spotted Jamie's car parked on the side of the road. She slowed, turned off the road into the set of slushy black tire tracks he'd left behind, and parked behind his car, but he wasn't inside. She opened her car door, stepped into the icy thrust of lake wind, scanning the cove below: an easy crescent, rimmed by huge, tree-furred headlands—dark basalt jutting into the frozen lake like circling arms.

She had been here before.

There were footprints in the snow, and she followed them onto the path that led to the beach, icy grass crunching underfoot as she made her way toward the eastern headland. The footprints led to an ancient Sitka spruce that had grown out of the hillside. At some point in the last few centuries, the ground underneath the spruce had opened in a wide fissure, and now the tree's sprawling roots reached to straddle both sides.

She knew this place, knew that the fissure under the spruce roots was wide enough to fit through, and that it dropped into a rocky passageway that led to a network of caverns.

Nan had brought her here, after Evelyn had gone out one Friday night to find friends and stayed out until Monday morning—no phone call, no explanation. When she finally came home, Nan was sitting at the kitchen table, so still and silent that the only movement was the steam rising from the mug in her hands. When Nan looked at her, she could see what Nan saw: a porch dog. Evelyn hadn't thought to call—Jube had never asked her where she'd been. Staring at Nan from the open door, she was heavy with guilt. Nan had been waiting for her. And her first thought was to take a giant lurching step backward out of the house, shut the door, and run, because the weight of shame was too much to bear.

But Nan seemed to know exactly what she was thinking and sat up straighter, smiled at her, and said, "Were you out all these nights dancing with a prince at the underground lake?"

Evelyn blinked. "What?"

Nan stood up. "I'll show you."

Nan got dressed and drove Evelyn to the north shore, led

her to this exact Sitka spruce, to the crevice underneath that they had to sidle through. Nan had brought a flashlight and she turned it on, shining the beam on the narrow passageway.

"Watch your head."

And Evelyn understood: Nan was trying to keep her. Evelyn was drifting away like a buoy and Nan was trying to hold on to her with everything she had.

Together, they moved through the elemental dark. Nan seemed to know exactly where she was going—seemed to have come here before.

"Nan, listen. I'm sorry," Evelyn said. Her voice sounded close in the darkness, as if speaking to a wall. "I should've called." The air grew colder the farther they went.

"Once upon a time, there was a king who had twelve daughters," Nan said. "The king had a problem. Every night, he locked his twelve daughters in their room, and every morning they were tired, almost impossible to wake up, and their slippers were worn through as if they'd been dancing all night."

Nan crouched low and held onto the rock wall as she toed the slope that dropped into shadow. She stepped down carefully and then turned to help Evelyn. Nan panned the flashlight over twisting, reaching stalagmites and dripping stalactites, the whole forming a wide, black maw, everywhere the smell of old rock and earth and water.

"The king promised his kingdom to any man who could discover where the princesses were going each night, and a soldier volunteered. That night, he was locked in the princesses' room and pretended to be asleep, then secretly followed them through a trap door and down a tunnel to three groves of trees: one with leaves of silver, the next with leaves of gold, and the third with leaves of diamonds."

Nan guided Evelyn deeper into the cave, into a network of

rooms and passageways, disorienting in all its sameness. As they went farther, they came upon huge, thick columns that glittered when the flashlight beam passed over them.

"The princesses followed the tunnel to the shore of an underground lake where twelve princes were waiting for them in twelve boats. The princes rowed the princesses across the lake to a castle waiting on the other shore, and they went inside and danced all night long."

They were going farther down, deeper underground. Evelyn followed Nan nervously, gripping Nan's hand tight when they edged around a black hole that could have been a four-foot drop or a two-hundred-foot drop.

There was light up ahead, and they followed it until they came to a cavern the size of a ballroom, the ceiling thirty feet high with a wide-open hole at the top, through which smoky, gray light shone down on the black water before them. It was an underground lake—a lake under a lake. Evelyn couldn't see the other side of it.

The water sat calm, tannin black. The cavern smelled ancient.

"How deep is it?" Evelyn had asked. "How far does it go?"

"A hundred feet deep. A mile across," said Nan, sweeping the flashlight beam over the surface. "The old soldier took a gold cup from the underground castle and brought it back to the king with the leaves from the gold, silver, and diamond trees, as proof that he had been to the underground kingdom. He then married the king's oldest daughter and the twelve princes were cursed for as many nights as they had spent dancing with the princesses."

Now, as Evelyn crunched across the frozen grass toward the spruce, she looked out over the lake—half thawed since the storm, ice creeping toward the middle, as translucent as cooling wax.

The landslide had buried most of the south shore and the town didn't try to dig itself out, just rebuilt right on top of it. When Evelyn came down to the water's edge, she imagined churches, homes, stores right under her feet—an underground world where people still danced in a phosphorescent twilight.

Someone was coming out of the cave, surfacing in the light beneath the Sitka roots.

A branch cracked above her, a quick, pivoting motion, and a small gray bird shot out of the tree. When Evelyn looked up, she slipped on the ice, the dull, internal crack of her skull hitting something hard. Basalt. Ancient cooled lava.

In another moment, Jamie was crouching beside her.

"Jesus," he said. "What are you doing out here?"

She tried to sit up but her head swam. She lay back down and focused her vision on the pine canopy. She was wet—clothes, hair, skin—and her fingertips and lips were numb. She was shivering, teeth chattering. Her head ached like a hangover.

"Can you move?" Jamie asked.

Evelyn tried again to sit up, but a cresting wave of nausea made her lie back down. She felt Jamie's hand on her shoulder. When she looked up, she saw Jamie, eyes large, aureoles of gold around the wells of his pupils.

"Okay. Come on," he said, hooking an arm around her ribcage and helping her to her feet.

Her head swung, and her legs shivered and gave out. Jamie steadied his weight to guide her through the frozen ferns and grass and back to the road. He was leading her to his car.

"I gotta go home," she said.

Jamie looked at her. "Like this?" He opened the passenger's-side door. "You need to go to the hospital."

"I can't go to a hospital."

"You have a concussion."

"No insurance," she said.

Jamie's mouth tightened but he didn't say anything more as he lowered her into his car and she sank into the familiarity of it. He got into the driver's side and sat quietly for a moment, gripping the wheel, thinking—but Evelyn was already feeling her head slip away, and before he'd even put the car in drive, she was asleep.

She opened her eyes and saw him driving, his right arm braced on the wheel—sturdy, a cedar bough. Her eyes closed. When they opened again, the car had stopped in front of a sprawling, brick Tudor-style house—enormous—dizzying in its spread as she struggled to locate the house's focal point. Where was the front door? At least three gabled facades crawling with ivy loomed over rolling swells of green lawn. Manicured topiaries lined the breezeways, and a turret glowered over the grounds, complete with ramparts. The whole house looked out over the expanse of the lake.

She turned to Jamie. He was staring at the house grimly. He looked at her.

"Come on," he said, grabbing his gym bag from the floor and opening his door.

He helped her out of the car and they approached the house—huge, formidable, smelling like musty vines. He helped her up the porch steps and opened the front door, and the first thing she saw was the swirling sweep of a staircase, wide, glittering, forking at the first landing and then spreading its arms to opposite sides of the house. Glossy hardwood floors gleaming white in the window light. A glass vase of roses atop a narrow wrought iron stand. The house was cold. No one home. But as Jamie held her with one arm around her waist, her arm around his neck, he scanned the room, mouth tight, looking for something, someone.

"Is this your house?" Evelyn asked.

Jamie puffed out a short, bitter laugh. "No."

He led her down a hallway to the left, at the end of which was a white living room—white walls, white sofas and armchairs, white carpet. Instead of taking her to the living room, he opened a door to a bedroom—white, just like the other room. The bedroom was strangely small for the size and sprawl of the house, and the bed took up most of the space, so it felt like they were huddling in a closet together.

He lowered her onto the bed and set his gym bag beside her, unzipping it. She could instantly smell the heady mix of his scent and pool water. He took out a folded set of clothes—sweatpants and T-shirt.

"Here. Some dry clothes until we can figure out what to do with you," he said, handing them to her.

"I'll be fine in a few minutes. I need to get home to my kids," she said, wincing. Her head throbbed and her vision was still drifting. She squeezed her eyes shut to steady herself.

"You have kids?" Jamie asked.

"Two," said Evelyn. "Girls." Stopping herself before she handed over any more information.

She opened her eyes and Jamie was looking at the floor, rubbing the back of his head, as if he were the one that had fallen.

"I'll let you get changed," he said before leaving.

When the door clicked shut, Evelyn stood up unsteadily and undressed, taking off her wet bra and underwear before sliding like cold metal into the sweatpants and T-shirt. Nothing between her skin and Jamie's clothes. She felt close to him, like she used to when she put on Packy's clothes—rolling in him.

She was tilting and she grabbed onto the dresser to find her balance just as Jamie rapped a knuckle on the door and opened it. He was suddenly behind her, hands on her waist.

"Are you okay?" he asked. "Evelyn?"

"Yeah." She righted herself. "Just dizzy."

The room was dark, lit solely by the silvery light coming through the window. Jamie took his hands off her.

"You can stay here tonight," he said. "I'll take the guest room next door."

"Whose house is this?" Evelyn asked.

Jamie picked up his gym bag and said, "They won't be home until Monday."

"I can't stay."

Jamie rubbed his eyes. "Fine. At least eat something and then I'll drive you back to your car."

"Fine."

"Stay here. I'll get something from the kitchen."

He left and Evelyn sank back down to the bed. Before she tipped sideways, she wondered if she should call home to tell Nan she'd be late.

She fell into a half-sleep stillness—neither awake nor asleep, but unable to move, like the times she'd fallen asleep in Jamie's car. She didn't dream, but rather remembered. The time Lila fell off a chair in the kitchen and Evelyn jumped up to go to her, but Erin—home from her year-long absence—got to her first. Waking in the morning to find Erin making Mickey Mouse pancakes for Lila and Mora, smiling down her shoulder at them. The fear shimmering in Erin's eyes like asphalt heat when Mora cried and reached for Evelyn.

She remembered the night she came home from work and Lila pushed away from Erin and Doris on the couch to grab Evelyn's hand in both of hers and say, "I hungry," because it was eight thirty and no one had made dinner for her yet. Evelyn went into the kitchen to get Lila a graham cracker, having learned that when Lila said she was hungry, she needed to eat something at that exact moment in order to head off a panicking tantrum.

Erin followed, got a pot out of the cupboard and began filling it with water.

"How about some macaroni and cheese?" she asked Lila.

Lila didn't answer, crushing the graham cracker in her mouth and then turning her big eyes up to Evelyn for another one. Evelyn handed her another from the box and then put the rest in the pantry. Lila broke her second cracker in half, then into quarters, and began eating the quarters one at a time, methodically. Erin was watching Lila.

"Why's she doin that?" Erin asked, watching Lila. "Why's she breakin em like that?"

"She always eats em that way. She eats the first one real fast. She's choked a few times. And then she breaks the second one up into little pieces and eats em slow."

Both women watched as Lila took small, pecking bites out of the graham cracker quarters.

"I only let her have two crackers before a meal," Evelyn explained, but she could see from Erin's slack mouth and distant eyes that she wasn't listening.

Erin went back to the pot of water, which wasn't going to boil because she hadn't put a lid on it yet. She rubbed her forehead. "I know I fucked up," she said quietly. Her voice had a slight southern roll. "I know they love you now and call you Mama. But—" She was thin, her tank top loose so that the straps kept slipping down her sharp shoulders. "I had to get out of here to get clean. I couldn't be their mama and get clean at the same time."

And Evelyn had nodded as if she understood.

When she woke up, she couldn't tell what time it was. The room was dark and she was lying in the strange white bed, head on a pillow that smelled like lake water, bedspread pulled up over her shoulder. There was no clock in the room. She sat up and a blooming nimbus of pain opened in her skull. She felt her pockets for her phone, already knowing that it wouldn't be there.

She threw back the covers and stood up, vision flickering white. She found her clothes hanging on the bed frame and checked her jeans, but her phone wasn't there either. She went to the closed door, opened it, peered down the dark hallway. There was no light, except for a faint blue cast under the staircase. She quietly made her way out to the living room, turned on the light—a brilliant flourish of pain behind her eye sockets—switched it off again, and continued back down the hall toward the staircase, following the blue light to a dining room. She flipped on the light, squinted through the crushing ache, and saw that just like the living room and the bedroom she'd slept in, the dining room was all white except for a glossy black banquet table, smooth and cold under her fingers. She moved into the kitchen—industrial, utilitarian, with white tile and glittering chrome countertops. Past the kitchen, the sitting room—all white with soaring floor-to-ceiling windows that looked out over the midnight-blue lake.

There was enough light in the sky to make out the glassy sheen of ice, the mountains in the mist. She turned on the light and the lake disappeared and she was staring at her own reflection floating in white—an erasure, an absence. That was when she saw the family portrait on the wall behind her: a doughy-faced man with glasses, thick hair, and unnaturally straight, white teeth; a woman with white-blonde hair and soft eyes, a kind, maternal smile—Ursula. Blank-faced between them: McKenzie.

They were in Ursula's house.

Beside the family portrait was a black-and-silver numberless clock. Five in the morning, with no call home the night before.

Evelyn moved swiftly back the way she came, through the kitchen, the dining room, past the staircase to the bedroom, flipping on the light switch. She would change, wake Jamie, and make him drive her back to her car. She must have left her phone in there. She would call Nan and then race home.

She took off the T-shirt and sweatpants and grabbed her musty damp jeans off the bed frame, but when she turned, she saw Jamie standing in the open doorway. His eyes were large and he had one hand on the doorknob. They stared at one another, an edge of fear in his eyes that was slowly smoothing into a calcium glitter: wonder. He sighed.

She was the first one to blink, to clip the tendon stretched taut between them, and Jamie quickly turned to face the wall as Evelyn grabbed her damp clothes and dressed. They didn't speak, but as Evelyn stepped into her jeans, she could see the underside of his jaw, his eyelashes, blinking, looking down at the floor—smiling. When she was done dressing, they left the house wordlessly and went out to his car. Evelyn got in first, and as Jamie opened his door, she saw the stain on the driver's seat, still there, now a faded earth-brown smear.

NAN

The only reason Nan knew Evelyn was gone was because she woke up to Clara's voice and her hunched shadow sitting at the foot of the bed where Rosie usually lay, hands on her knees, hawk nose pointing at the wall ahead of her as she spoke in a low, tired voice. Nan couldn't understand what she was saying. "What? Clara, what are you doing here? It's the middle of the night." Nan propped herself up on one elbow. "Where's Rosie? Rosie," she called. The dog lifted her head where she was lying on the floor at the foot of the bed.

"You let me borrow your house dresses because back then they didn't make clothes for pregnant women," Clara said. "You had to take them out yourself and you knew how to sew. I didn't. I probably could've asked my mother but she didn't have no time—just trying to keep the seams of her own dresses together while she was scrubbing floors on her hands and knees in those white rubber shoes she wore because they were comfortable and clean lookin. Didn't leave no scuff marks." Clara's voice was even but worn down, as if she'd been walking all day without rest. "I knew we were poor when I went to Mamie Jericho's house and saw the beautiful cake her mother had made her—yellow cake with pink frosting and piped roses. She made Mamie's party dress too, that pink one with the satin flower on the shoulder. All the things she'd made for Mamie's party, I knew she didn't need my mother to come over once a week to clean her house. She didn't work, she had time. She churned her own butter for God's sake. She had my mother clean her house to give her work. Your mother did the same thing."

"Clara, what's the matter with you?"

Clara was quiet, and then she turned to Nan in the darkness. A tuft of hair had sprung loose over her left ear.

"You know what really surprised him when he went into the lake," she said, eyes shining, "was that he could breathe the water."

Nan sat up but realized that the sheets were soaked through and cold. Her nightgown was wet. She switched on her bedside lamp and threw back the covers to find herself in a spreading ellipse of blood—dark and deep, a plunging pit in her bed. Her nightgown clung to her skin, soaked through.

Her breath became a thick mucus in her throat as she jerkily stumbled out of the room, trying to call out for Evelyn but unable to make sound. She staggered down the hall to Evelyn's open door, but when she came to the bed she saw only the girls, right where she had left them: Mora in her expansive X, Lila curled on her side facing the wall with Mora's fist in the crook of her neck. No Evelyn.

The earthy menstrual smell was thick and she could feel a swoon coming as she made her way heavy-footed to the bathroom. She flipped on the light and looked in the mirror—no blood. Her nightgown was dry and spotless. She stared, rubbing her eyes with trembling fingers, and looked again. Nothing. Breathless and heart flapping, she went to her bedroom to find her sheets clean and dry as well, nothing of the violence of before.

She stood beside her bed for several minutes, trying to steady her breathing, and then put on her slippers and robe and went out to the living room, hearing the slow clicking of Rosie's claws as the dog followed her in achy exhaustion. Nan started a pot of coffee and then peeked through the curtain over the front window. Evelyn's car was gone. The clock on the oven read 4:42 a.m., and Nan tried to remember if Evelyn was working a night shift—if Evelyn had come home at all last night.

When the coffee was done, she poured herself a cup, opened the curtains, and sat down at the table to look at the moonless dark. Rosie flopped down on her feet under the table.

That was where she was when Evelyn's splotchy red Corolla pulled onto the gravel driveway sometime after sunrise and Evelyn got out, harried, frowning. She walked with a stoop in her hurry to get in the front door, and when she came in with a blast of winter air and her eyes met Nan's, she asked, "Why didn't you pick up the phone?" She was breathless, lips flushed pink, eyes clear, like she'd been running in the cold. "I been callin. Didn't you hear the phone ring?"

"The phone didn't ring," said Nan.

And both women looked at the phone on the wall, as if it would explain itself. Evelyn crossed the room and took the phone off the receiver, putting it to her ear, and Nan could hear the dial tone from the table. Evelyn hung up and took her phone out of her pocket, dialing. A moment later, the home phone rang, and Evelyn looked at Nan with—grim annoyance? Exasperation?

"What's that look?" Nan asked.

Evelyn shook her head and put her phone back in her pocket. "No look." She peeked out the window for a moment at the silver-blue dawn, before she turned to Nan. "Are the girls still asleep?"

Nan felt an itch at her neck under her jaw and scratched it. The skin was dry and patchy, the beginnings of a rash. She felt a seep of wetness.

"You okay?" asked Evelyn.

"Yeah. Just this hot spot on my neck."

Evelyn squinted at it. "Don't scratch. It'll get infected."

Nan threw her hands up with a teasing huff. She flashed a smile at Evelyn. "Go on and get some rest. You can sleep in my bed so the girls don't wake you up."

"I'm okay, actually. I'm gonna do some work around here. I never finished putting in the downspouts on the back of the house," said Evelyn. She looked at Nan with a crooked smile, concerned. "You sure you're okay?"

Nan intertwined her fingers over her chin and smiled at her.

The snowmelt left foamy, gray slush in the ruts on the road. Nan wrapped scarves around the little girls' faces—pressing one finger down underneath their noses to leave enough of a gap for them to breathe—and buckled them into their car seats to go to the grocery store. Every year, she went food shopping on December twenty-third to get the turkey and fixings. On Christmas Eve, she went back for rolls so they wouldn't be stale by Christmas Day, as she'd done every year since she married Earl—even the years after Evelyn had left.

There was only one grocery store on the south shore and everyone in town was there to do their Christmas dinner shopping. The aisles were packed with old women and men bumping shopping carts, and Nan had to put Lila in the cart basket to keep her from getting run over. In the years when she'd come to the grocery store to shop for her own Christmas dinner, she'd seen the looks on the faces around her—the people who knew she was alone, who knew she was cooking for no one. It made her embarrassingly aware of her aloneness.

She spotted Myrna at the front of the store and walked past her without saying hello. In the produce section, she saw Linney Bradford, who glanced up at her before quickly turning back to the green apples she was bagging.

Nan picked up a twelve-pound Butterball, along with stuffing mix, onions, celery, and marshmallows. She pushed the cart to the canned food aisle but got there at the same time as Myrna. Their eyes met and Myrna twisted her mouth into a defiant sneer, raised her eyebrows, and rolled her eyes theatrically. Nan shoved her cart forward and said, "Trash."

She went to the baking section for cans of pumpkin puree and a bag of sugar, the coolers for eggs and cream. As she grabbed a box of butter, she spotted Myrna again, staring back at her with a tub of sour cream in her hands. Nan lifted her chin and pushed her cart past, but not before hearing Myrna say quietly, "Thief." Nan whipped around, but Myrna was already walking away, back straight.

Nan woke up early Christmas morning—still dark—to start cooking, and came out to the kitchen to find Evelyn sitting at the table, drinking a cup of coffee. Evelyn smiled weakly and said, "What do you need me to do?"

"The apples."

Evelyn finished her coffee and then went to the sink, rinsed her mug, and got the apples out of the fridge. While she peeled,

Nan got the potatoes from the pantry and began peeling and dicing. She put them in a pot of water to boil, and by the time the sun was tipping the pines red, the windows were fogged with steam. Lila and Mora both came staggering into the kitchen barefoot and bleary-eyed at eight—holding hands, which made Nan and Evelyn sigh.

They opened presents: a plastic scooter for Lila that Evelyn found at a yard sale, a squeaking and chattering toy camera for Mora. Nan and Evelyn didn't exchange gifts because they never had. They ate a simple breakfast of oatmeal so that they could focus on the bigger meal ahead, and the house came alive with cooking smells. When the turkey was ready at one o'clock, Nan set the table while Evelyn carved.

As they were sitting down to eat, Jubilee's old, blue hatchback bobbled up the road. Nan and Evelyn watched from the front window as Jube veered onto the lawn without slowing down, two snapping Chihuahuas jumping and rolling across the back window. She parked and got out with the dogs tumbling after her, and then she reached in and brought out a small Tupperware container. She threw a studded, black corduroy purse over her shoulder, grabbed a pot of begonias off the seat, and hiked up the porch steps.

Evelyn and Nan looked at one another—not just the question of why Jube was there or whether they should open the door, but who would make the call. Evelyn stared at Nan unblinking because it was Nan's house so she had to make the decision, but Nan simply took Lila's plate and busied herself with serving food, asking, "How about some turkey?"

Evelyn went to the door just as Jube knocked. Jube smiled her panting-dog smile and held up the Tupperware container as she said, "I brought your favorite mashed potatoes with the sour cream and garlic."

Evelyn took the container and stepped aside as Jube took the last heaving step into the house. The Chihuahuas yapped as they scurried around the living room, barking Rosie into a corner as she whined nervously. And then, seeing the table with Nan and the two girls, the little dogs broke into a firing report of barks.

"Just put them in the bathroom," Jube yelled over the barking as she set the potted begonias on the kitchen counter.

Evelyn clapped her hands at the little dogs and tried to guide them down the hall, but they hopped and yapped at her.

"Dot! Izzy! Go lay down!" Jube yelled, herding them down the hallway to the door Evelyn held open. Once the dogs were inside, Evelyn closed the door quickly, which only slightly damped the noise.

"Duke died and Paulie got me these two from a old lady who lives down the street. I know they're loud but they're the sweetest little babies," said Jube as she and Evelyn reemerged into the living room. "Woof, hot in here," she said as she sloughed her purse onto the couch and unbuttoned her sweater.

Evelyn looked at Nan, and Nan got out of her chair.

"Sit here," she said. "It's cooler by the window."

Jube took the offered chair. Evelyn gave Nan her own seat and got the collapsible step stool out of the pantry to sit on. Nan took up a serving spoon and asked, "Green beans?" Jube held out her plate.

Jube took a few bites and then set her knife and fork down. "Those cute grandbabies of mine look so delicious, I might just eat them instead of the turkey," she said, and then wheezed out a laugh. Lila and Mora stared at her with wide, unswerving eyes.

Nan tried not to look at Evelyn—didn't want Evelyn to be embarrassed for Jube. They could still hear the barks in the bathroom. Mora and Lila were both staring at the hallway, as if waiting for the dogs to appear.

"I bet you make tuna sandwiches with Miracle Whip for them little ones," Jube said to Nan. "Remember those? How you used to make those for me? On white bread?"

Nan nodded and smiled without making eye contact as she cut Lila's food.

"Miracle Whip?" said Evelyn, looking at Nan.

"Oh. Nan got me hooked on it as a kid. Almost every day, I could walk across the street and she'd have a tuna sandwich waiting for me—white bread, no crust. Now I can *only* eat tuna with Miracle Whip." She laughed. "She also got me hooked on the newspaper without meanin to. Remember how Dad used to take it from you in the morning and bring it back after breakfast?"

Jube laughed a chesty laugh but Nan's smile was strained, remembering how often she'd go outside to get the newspaper only to find it missing. Later, drinking her coffee at the table, she'd see Royce through the kitchen window, crossing the street with the unrolled newspaper in hand. If she didn't go out and meet him in the yard, he'd simply leave the loose pages on her doorstep, not even bothering to tuck them under the mat so they wouldn't fly away.

"I read it with him sometimes. He gave me the cartoons."

"I never seen you eat a tuna sandwich," Evelyn said to Nan. "I didn't know you liked tuna. Or Miracle Whip."

Nan shrugged. "I never felt like buying a whole tub of Miracle Whip just for one tuna sandwich. Because what else can you do with Miracle Whip?"

With nothing else to say, Evelyn fell silent and focused her attention on Mora, spooning a small heap of mashed potatoes into the baby's mouth. Mora smacked her lips once and then gagged, eyes watering as the mash slid out of her mouth and onto her tray. Evelyn wiped Mora's chin with the heel of her palm and then wiped her hand on her jeans.

"You know. These girls really don't look a thing like you," Jube said to Evelyn.

Evelyn paused, eyes alert—and in her stillness, the differences between her and the two girls seemed to stand out in relief. Her dark hair, black-tunnel eyes, squared jaw, then Lila and Mora: round-faced and blue-white.

"I don't look like you either," said Evelyn.

And she was right. Jube shrugged. Jube had nothing of her own mother, and they could all see the chalk-yellow hair she had inherited from her father, along with his hard, thin lips and bull shoulders. She pushed her turkey around on her plate, swirled it in mashed potatoes, dipped it in some gravy, and forked it into her mouth, chewing loudly. Nan closed her eyes, breathed through her nose, and tried not to let Evelyn see her annoyance, because if anyone knew how much smacking-food noises bothered Nan, it was Evelyn.

Jube set down her fork and cleared her throat. "I left Paulie," she said.

Evelyn didn't say anything as she ate her green beans.

"Just this morning," Jube added. "We had a fight."

Jube paused. She opened her mouth to say something, but then shook her head and waved her hand. Evelyn glanced at her briefly before returning to her plate.

"I got nowhere to go," said Jube.

Evelyn's eyes flicked up, incredulous. "That's *your* house. You had it before you even met Paulie."

"I know," Jube said with exasperation. "I told him to leave and he said no. He said his job pays the mortgage—"

"Mortgage? I thought that thing was paid off already."

"We refinanced a few years ago to get Paulie's new truck and install a slider in the master bedroom—and we were really glad we had it when we got Dot and Izzy because them two need to go out all hours of the night." Jube waved her hand again, ignoring Evelyn's groan. "It's just that—he ain't gonna leave. I got nowhere else to go."

The table was silent. Nan looked from Jube to Evelyn, who kept her eyes on her plate as she ate.

"Can I stay here for a while?" asked Jube.

"No," said Evelyn.

"Until I get something more stable set up," Jube said, not hearing Evelyn.

"No," Evelyn said again.

They went silent. Jube was looking at Evelyn and then turned to Nan, who stared back uncomprehending. Evelyn set down her fork hard and looked at Jube.

"No," she said again, as if Jube hadn't heard her.

"I raised you!—"

"Go find somewhere else to stay."

Jube jerked her head in affronted alarm. Her fingers tapped the table, but she didn't make any move to stand.

"I'll get your dogs," said Evelyn, rising.

There was a brief rabble of scudding chairs and barking dogs, slamming doors, the rev of Jube's car and the wheels tearing out of the front yard. When Evelyn came back to the table, her shoulders and neck were tight and she wouldn't look at Nan. The house was silent again, except for the scrape of Evelyn's knife.

"That might've been unnecessarily harsh," Nan finally said, and Evelyn's dark eyes flashed. "Look," Nan said, taking her napkin off her lap and folding it on the table. "Jubilee is a . . . rough woman. She had a mean father—mean, mean man. She lost her mother when she was very young."

"I know all that. She's a grown woman. We can't blame our childhoods for everything," Evelyn said. "She's gotta answer for herself just like I do."

Evelyn didn't say anything more, didn't look at Nan again as she ate her food and took her plate to the sink. She got a dishtowel out of the drawer, dampened it under the trickling faucet, and brought it back to the table to wipe Mora's face. But as she was wiping the baby's fat pink hands, she glanced out the window and froze. An almost imperceptible shift of fear passed through her face like an insect flashing in the dark, and she whispered something—"Erin"—as she lurched for the front door. In another moment, she was outside, hands braced on the porch rail, staring at the half-frozen mud road—at nothing. Nan got to her just as Evelyn turned and fixed her eyes on a small mangled bird impaled on a jutting nail on the porch post. Evelyn stared, mouth bobbing open and shut.

"Erin, Erin . . ." she whispered, then covered her mouth.

"What?" said Nan. She looked at the bird. "That? That's a dark-eyed junco."

"Erin did that," Evelyn said.

"No she didn't. A northern shrike did that. That's a shrike larder."

Evelyn stared at her. "What?" Her voice piano-wire tight, a quiver.

"The northern shrike kills its prey and then impales it on a twig or a thorn of some sort to save it for later. It's called a shrike larder. They're all over the place." Nan sighed, breath smoking in the winter sun, and rubbed Evelyn's arm. "Erin isn't here. Come back inside."

The gas station mini-mart was closed for Christmas, but Evelyn had to go in at midnight to work the night shift. Nan never heard her moving through the house, but she could see the kitchen light on at ten. By the time Nan came out to make her coffee at five, Evelyn was gone, leaving behind no trace of herself.

Nan took out the quart mason jar of marshmallow tea she'd left steeping in the fridge overnight, strained it, and mixed in a little sugar to have it ready for Lila, whose cough had loosened but still occasionally left her twisted and gasping. This was the last of the marshmallow root and the nebulizer only temporarily opened her airways.

Lila and Mora toddled sleepily out of their bedroom at seven. At eight, the sun rose somewhere on the other side of the silver cloud cover. At eight thirty, there was a knock at the door and Nan knew it was Jube before she opened it. Jube stood on the porch, hair wisping crazily out of her ponytail and nostrils pink and raw from the cold.

"I left my begonias," she said grimly.

Nan held the door open and let her in.

Jube didn't ask for coffee but Nan poured some anyway, and then took the lid off a Tupperware container of shortbread cookies she'd made days earlier and set everything out on the table. Jube had already sat down in the same spot by the window. When Nan set her mug down, Jube picked it up and slurped her coffee, and Nan could see the thin dusting of black hair on her upper lip.

"I did my best by her. You gotta talk to Evelyn and tell her that," Jube said, not looking at Nan as she slurped again.

"I did. I do," said Nan. "I know you did your best."

"She wasn't easy. She could be mean—she bit people all the time. She bit Verne Holbrook in the face."

"What was he doing with his face so close to hers?"

"Fuck if I know! I'm sayin she was wild is what I'm sayin. She told lies—I could watch her pull the dog's ears or yank on his tail, and then she'd get bit and I'd say, 'Well what'd you expect, pullin his ears like that?' And she'd look me square in the face and say, 'I didn't pull his ears.'" Jube's eyes went wide and she flung her hands up in the air. "So what am I supposed to do?"

Nan sipped her coffee and didn't say anything.

"So then Paulie comes along and he's good for me. It'd been so long being just me and Evelyn, and then all a sudden I got this man who wants to take care of me and she can't stand it. She hated him the minute he walked through the door."

They both fell silent. Jube sipped her coffee and ate one of the shortbread cookies, nibbling the whole thing to nothing before she finally spoke again.

"She really was the cutest baby, though," she said with a distant smile. "So cute. Black hair and everything from her daddy. I breastfed her even though Grandma begged me not to, said it was what poor women did—even though she was poor as they come. And I said, 'What am I? Rich?' I'd go to feed her and Grandma—you remember Grandma Jeanne, Dad's mom. She watched Evie for me while I worked, gave her a bottle of milk with Karo syrup in it. When I'd come home and nurse her, Grandma Jeanne would call it 'Tittin the baby.' And that little baby was always so hungry—just couldn't get enough, even though I tried to make her wait because that's what the doctor said to do back then. Make em wait four hours between feedings. But that's because everybody bottle-fed and we didn't know that breastfed babies had to eat more often, did we? So she'd cry, and cry, and cry for hours, and I'd cry with her, begging her to wait a little bit longer."

Jube twisted her mouth to one side and huffed at the memory, and then her eyes met Nan's, because they were having the same thought: Nan had never fed a baby. The closest she came to motherhood was Peter.

In the living room, Lila coughed wetly—a popping,

bubbling cough—while she and Mora watched cartoons, sitting side by side on the rug with their heads tipped back to look up at the screen, backs rounded like breeching turtles.

Jube ate another cookie, and Nan realized that she never said thank you. Never said, "These are good," or "Thanks for the coffee," or even "Thanks for dinner yesterday," just like when she was little. Ate and drank like it was meant for her, and then ran home without even saying goodbye.

"You have this tiny baby and you fall in love with her, and she's so in love with you," Jube sighed. "And then one day, she's gone, and there's a bratty kid in her place, throwin tantrums and biting you and tellin you she hates you. After Paulie come along she said she didn't love me no more. But I always thought to myself, 'Don't I have a right?' After everything I did for her—she tore me from one hole to the other just comin out. All the time I spent feedin her, gettin up with her in the night, worryin myself sick every time she coughed, spendin my whole paycheck on diapers and baby food. Don't I have a right to her love?"

Jube was looking at Nan now, a question in her stare. A demand.

"I don't know if we have a right to anyone's love," said Nan, lowering her coffee.

Jube was quiet for a minute, and then puffed out a bitter laugh—loud enough to make Nan jump.

"You *would* say somethin like that," Jube said with a grim smile. "Probably makes you feel better." She took the last short-bread cookie and bit half of it off, mouth full and smacking. "You think you *earned* her love, don't you? Worked harder'n me for it?"

Nan sighed. "No, Jube. That's not what I meant. I meant that none of us can really feel entitled to another person's feelings—"

"Why can't I? Little babies need love to grow. Even with all the milk in the world, if they don't got no one to love em and hold em, they don't grow—they die. I gave her *all* my love." She jabbed her thumb into her chest. "And I got a right to be loved back. You think love didn't get you where you are in life? You didn't raise yourself," Jube said when Nan opened her mouth to speak. "You didn't go to school and get a education by yourself. Your parents gave you everything. And when you didn't get something, you took it. You didn't get into this house by yourself. You took it from Clara." Nan felt her jaw tighten, and Jube smiled, seeing that she'd found the exposed nerve. "Oh yeah. Don't think nobody knows that one. Everyone knows what you did. It was before my time but even *I* know that she took you in when your husband left, and that you lived in her house while she was workin in the camp—and that *you* gave her boy to the doctor. And course everyone knows you went to his house every chance you got. Probably thought you were going to be a little family." Jube pointed a yellow-nailed finger at Nan's face. "My mother warned me to stay away from you, said, 'Don't go to that house because she'll take you from me.' But I didn't listen to her. Maybe if I did, you wouldn't've taken my girl."

And before Nan knew what she was doing, she'd lunged across the table and slapped Jube in the face.

"Get out of my house," she said in a faltering, breathless voice.

But in one quick motion, Jube pushed herself from the table and lurched at Nan, who jerked back so that Jube's fist only batted at her collarbone. Coffee mugs and plates crashed to the floor as Jube pulled herself forward by yanking on the tablecloth, then lunged again for Nan, this time snarling her fingers in Nan's shirt so that both women tumbled to the ground. Jube straddled Nan and attempted to hit her in the face, but Nan got one hand on Jube's fleshy chin and pushed it as far back as she

140

could, so that Jube was fighting against her own chin.

That was how Evelyn found them. Nan hadn't heard her come in—just heard her yell, "—the fuck?" And then Evelyn was grabbing Jube under the armpits and dragging her away—impossible strength in her wiry arms. In another moment, Jube's thick-shouldered body was tumbling down the porch steps and Evelyn was slamming the front door shut as Jube yelled, "My begonias!"

The house was quiet again, save for the chatter of the cartoons.

Air bright with wood smoke, Nan waded carefully through the slushy puddle that had flooded the dip in Linden Road, and then hiked up the incline on the other side. Her slacks were wet from pushing through the thawing ferns, and all around her, the pine trees were sloughing off clumps of ice and snow that fell in thick plops on the forest floor.

She and Evelyn hadn't spoken of Jube. After she'd come in, Evelyn made herself a sandwich with the leftover turkey, and then sat down at the table and ate in silence. When she was done, she went into the bathroom and took a shower.

That night, Nan had woken up when she heard the crunch of tires on the gravel outside, saw the flash of headlights swiveling across the wall. She'd gone out to the dark living room, where Evelyn was already standing at the window in her jeans and jacket, waiting to start her shift at the gas station. By the time Nan reached the window, the car was gone, red taillights glowing down the street.

"Jube?" Nan had said.

"Mm-hmm," Evelyn sighed.

Nan looked at Evelyn for a long time and opened her mouth

to ask, "Did I steal you? Did I take you from her?" But it wasn't fair to make Evelyn answer, just to lighten Nan's guilt.

Now, Nan crested the hill and smelled the rhododendrons—no blooms, but the memory of the scent lingering like an old exhalation. She kept her eyes down so she wouldn't see the house that had gone to seed, steadily decomposing into its riparian origins—the house that she once thought she'd live in with the surgeon. Nothing left of the Tooley family that built the house. Nothing left of the surgeon, who, like Peter, was somewhere at the bottom of the lake.

Except when she raised her eyes, there he was, hands in pockets, shoulders squared, standing in front of the house that was stark white and imposing among the cedars and firs. He was staring back at her and her throat closed. Still achingly handsome with eyes like chipped ice.

"Back for more marshmallow root?" he asked, smiling.

"It worked," said Nan, smiling back at him. "I didn't think it would do anything, but it did." She tucked a lock of lank hair behind her ear, too aware of her haggard appearance, her bloodless face and hands, long teeth. "Peter's cough has cleared up so much. I can't believe it." Her head swam and she had to squeeze her eyes shut to steady herself. Still bleeding from the stillbirth, she was weak, straining to hear over the throbbing in her ears. It had sapped her completely to pull the sled up the hill to the doctor's house, and now Peter sat quietly, leaning back in his nest of blankets, breathing slowly and deeply, which meant he'd fallen asleep.

Only days earlier, she'd held him all night while he coughed and caught his breath in sharp, whooping gasps, holding him upright on her lap because that was the only way he could get air. Holding him even as she felt blood slushing into her underwear, soaking through her nightgown. No one to mourn with her. No baby, no husband, no Clara. Caring for a toddler who wasn't hers in a house that wasn't hers. She hadn't spoken to another person in over a week, and she knew as soon as she looked in the doctor's cut-glass eyes that she'd come for no other reason than to talk to someone.

The surgeon tipped his head toward the house. "Come in. Come have some coffee. It'll give me a chance to see Peter's progress."

Nan backed away from the ruins, from the withered and browned rhododendrons. She was alone, no wagon, no Peter.

But she could feel Linden's warm hand on hers.

When did he touch her hand?

Not her hand. Her knee. She was crying on the floor of her bedroom. It was dark. She hadn't turned on a lamp all day. She was treading water, trying to keep her nose and mouth above the surface, but her body was heavy and sinking, slow, slow, slow. There was a bottle of Miltown tablets on the dresser. She'd taken too many—too easy to simply keep swallowing, keep gulping down the dark water that was filling her throat. Sinking deeper and deeper, falling away from the water's swinging surface. She called him—said on the phone, "I'm going to die."

He was crouched on one knee in front of her, eyes shining in the dark as he said, "You're not going to die. But you need to rest." His eyes so clear as he said, "I'll take Peter for a while."

By the time Clara returned to the south shore, the doctor was already showing Peter at his house. There were signs up on the road and ads in newspapers in other towns: Come See the Boy Without a Face. In a few months' time, Linden would be granted permanent custody, and he and Peter would get on a train that wouldn't make it out of town.

Nan tripped backward over a rhododendron root and fell. She sat up, staring ahead at the ruined house, the tower—missing shingles, half of its windows boarded up. She stood and wiped the wet seat of her pants as she hurried away from the house, slipping down the mud bank and then lurching forward, a slow throb in her ears as she crashed through the ferns and the elder bushes, running—somewhere.

Running back from the surgeon's house the day after the train went into the water because she couldn't believe he was really in the lake. Panting, breathless as she charged through the woods, wondering why Clara wasn't here. Where was Clara?

Where was Clara?

But she already knew where Clara was, and now, as she passed through the basalt boulders that stood like twin eggs at the edge of the woods, hands pressed to cold black rock and lichen as they were fifty years ago, she was looking down at the town, at Main Street—at Clara standing in the middle of it. Just like before.

Clara, standing in the street and crying, crying because the town had taken her child from her, every single one of them—and her crying turned into a moaning, a grinding, an igneous yawn that separated into lapping multiples until it was a roaring. That was when Nan had felt the ground shifting beneath her feet. She watched as the hillside came alive, as the beast rolled its giant shoulder blade and sent cedars and firs shivering, sliding in one clean shelf to cover the town, the post office, the Catholic church, the Methodist church, the cars on Main Street, and Clara. Sweet Clara.

Nan felt the slimy algae under her hands as she caught her breath between the boulders. Her dear Clara.

As she stared down at Main Street, she spotted Jube's car, parked in front of the post office. From where she stood, she could see Jube inside, a heap of clothes piled on top of her in the driver's seat.

Nan carefully picked her way down the hillside, wedging her feet sideways in the mud to stay balanced, but it didn't stop her from slipping twice. Normally she would've been horrified to have mud on the seat of her pants, but she didn't think anything of it as she walked up to Jube's car and cupped her hands over the glass. Jube lay curled on her side. Curled up like the little girl on the front porch.

The Chihuahuas jumped onto Jube and started barking at Nan. Jube opened her eyes, red and hot, chin jutting as she stared straight at Nan. Then she twitched and yawned. She looked around uncertainly for a moment, and then pushed the dogs and the pile of clothes off herself, into the back seat. She started the car and rolled down the window.

"Get in. Let's go," she said.

Nan got in the car, and together they drove back to Nan's house.

EVELYN

The tension in the kitchen was a wire stretched to snapping. Nan stared at Jube hatefully from the counter, even though she was the one who brought Jube home. Jube had come in with her little yipping dogs and said to Nan, "I'm not putting them in the bathroom." And Nan said nothing. Jube went through the fridge and cupboards like she'd always lived there.

Nan slipped into Evelyn's room that first night, closed the door, and flattened herself against it as she said, "I can't believe that woman."

"Why'd you bring her here?" Evelyn had asked.

"She made me!" Nan snapped.

It had been three days and Evelyn stopped by the house after her night shift at the gas station to check on them before leaving for the country club. She found Nan sipping her coffee and glaring at Jube poisonously over the rim of her mug. Jube pretended not to notice. The two women were usually careful never to be in the same room together. If one was in a corner of the house, the other was in the opposite. Nan often waited in her room until Jube left the kitchen before coming out to get coffee. Together they balanced out the house as if it were teetering on top of a pin.

Evelyn picked up Mora and kissed her on the cheek, bent over Lila and blew raspberries in her neck until the little girl wheezed. She left them there and tried not to think about the awkward suspension of bitterness in the house as she drove to work at the club. Driving past the lake, frosty gray under the overcast sky, she could see coots bobbing in and out of the water as they dived for leeches and roe. A formation of Canada geese flew overhead and cormorants perched splayfooted on mossy logs along the side of the road, their heads tipped back on the awkward S-bend of their necks.

She hadn't spoken to Jamie since leaving Ursula's house before Christmas. She didn't have his phone number.

She worked through her shift with a crawling itch, a feeling of incompleteness—like there was more to be said.

Before she clocked out, she went to the staff room, to the filing cabinet full of waivers that parents had to fill out, and Evelyn found Ursula's waiver. She wrote the address on a fast-food napkin someone had left out. Ursula lived ten minutes away. She couldn't know for sure that Jamie would still be there, but it was the only address she had for him—her only chance at seeing him again.

She drove out of the parking lot and down the winding hillside, back up the eastern side, through the dense, black forest and mountain mist to the ivy-covered house with its snow-dusted topiaries and the iron-gray lake that sprawled behind it. Jamie's car sat alone in the cul-de-sac.

Evelyn drove down the long, twisting driveway and parked behind Jamie's car. She got out and approached the house. The front door was unlocked and the air was almost as cold inside as out. There was music coming from some distant corner of the house, but the curtains were drawn and the house was dark, shadowy. Evelyn already knew that Jamie was alone in the house as she followed the music to the dining room, but he wasn't there. She backtracked and moved quietly up the wide staircase, going left at the split, and trailing the music down a hallway to the only room with light. The bedroom had its own small foyer that opened to a pale blaze—white sleigh sofa with wide, sweeping arms, a narrow white table and chair under the open window, tall white armoire in the corner. There were sweeping floor-to-ceiling windows—a wall of glass that looked out over the lake. The only indication that it was a bedroom was the canopy bed on a dais in the middle of the room. The bed frame was wrought iron made to look like thick, twisting vines, with tiny leaves and a small thorny wreath at the center of the canopy.

Jamie was sitting on the bed with his back to her, and when he heard her come in, he didn't turn around, just quickly wiped his eyes and cheeks with the heel of his hand.

"They're not here," he said quietly, in a voice she didn't recognize—thick with despair.

"Where are they?" asked Evelyn. "When are they coming back?"

Jamie didn't answer as he stared out the windows at the lake. The view was unbroken and breathtaking—miles of lake and conifer spears, the pale-blue ghosts of the Olympic Mountains to the east.

"Where are they?" Evelyn asked louder.

Jamie said heavily, "She's having the baby."

She realized with confusion that he was wearing a tuxedo—complete with a silver bow tie that she could see in his reflection in the window—but it didn't fit. The suit was loose on him, rumpled. He looked ridiculous, like a little boy dressed up in his father's clothes.

Finally, Evelyn understood. "So then you and Ursula."

Jamie didn't answer.

They were both silent, and Evelyn pretended to be taking in the vastness of the room.

"We shouldn't be here," she said.

Jamie was ghostly still, staring out the window. And then he touched a dress lying on the bed beside him. She hadn't noticed it there.

"Let's go. Do you want to go somewhere?" Evelyn asked.

"You might as well put it on. She's got dozens like it," he said, turning and holding up the dress for her to see.

Evelyn stared at him, at the dress—a long-sleeved, black sheath. She didn't make a move toward him and he shook the dress at her.

"They won't be back tonight," he said.

Evelyn crossed the room to see the dress better. She touched it. Fine, smooth, oily material that she couldn't place. Clean lines. Versace. She'd never even held a Versace dress before, let alone worn one, and now she was more awestruck by the richness of it than the dress itself.

"What's he do?" she asked.

"It's her money. She's an heiress. A Stadler."

He didn't explain further because he knew she'd know the name. The Stadler Railcar Company.

She took the dress from Jamie and went into the first door she saw—a closet. She dressed in the dark. Straight neckline, three-quarter sleeves, fabric sliding slippery smooth along her skin, but it wasn't fitted. The belly was loose, because—she realized—it was a maternity dress. She came barefoot into the light and Jamie smiled. In the oversized tuxedo, he looked small and childish—adorable—large eyes shining.

"You look beautiful," he said.

Evelyn grabbed a throw pillow off the sofa and stuffed it under the dress. "Better?"

His face changed subtly, a relaxing of the muscles in his forehead, his cheeks. Desire. But it was artificial—the belly wasn't real—and she felt somehow invisible under his stare.

She turned to go back to the closet to take off the dress, but in another instant, he was behind her, hands on her shoulders—fingers open, pleading. She went still, feeling the space between them, his warmth, and then he came closer, a hot breath against her neck.

"Please stay," he said.

He leaned his forehead against the back of her head. She could smell him—his sweat smell, detergent in his clothes, yeasty breath, but also a mineral smell. Water and rock.

A flicker of dread made her step away from him.

"You eat yet?" she asked.

She cooked dinner for him in his lover's kitchen, wearing his lover's dress. She kept the pillow underneath it the whole time and neither of them made any mention of it—both pretending not to notice, but he stared at her belly and she watched him staring. There was shrimp in the freezer, bow tie pasta in the pantry, fresh garlic, and butter. She sautéed the shrimp and boiled the pasta, thinking that if she were making dinner at home, it would've been macaroni and cheese or a tuna casserole. Nan knew how to cook shrimp, but Evelyn didn't, so it came out tough and chewy.

There was a wine cellar in the basement. Jamie went below and returned with an '89 Bordeaux.

"Won't they notice it missing?" asked Evelyn.

Jamie shrugged. "Sure, if they check the spreadsheet."

They ate at the sprawling dining room table as the sun set in a blaze of red behind the western hills, the valley flaring with golds and pinks. Sitting at opposite ends of the table, they didn't speak as they drank wine and speared shrimp. The house was painfully cold—the couple had turned off the heating when they left—and Evelyn could see her breath fogging in the air as she ate. She could see Jamie's breath fogging too. She was barefoot and the beds of her toenails had gone blue.

When they were finished, they washed their dishes and put them back in the cupboards so the kitchen would appear undisturbed.

They drank the last of the wine and Jamie held it up by the neck as he said, "I'll go put this in my car."

Evelyn nodded. "I should go. I can take it."

Jamie opened his mouth to speak, but nothing came out. Evelyn left him there and went back up the stairs to change. He followed her, and before she went into the bedroom, he said, "Stay."

Evelyn stopped and looked at him. They were both standing on the darkened landing.

"You could stay," he said. "They won't be back for a long time."

"I can't stay. I got kids," Evelyn said. "I can't play house in someone else's clothes all day."

Too far. His jaw set and his eyes hardened.

"I didn't mean it like that."

They stood in silence. Jamie didn't say anything as he moved past her and disappeared into the bedroom. She went in after him and found him sitting on the bed, his back to her, just as she'd found him earlier. The room was twilit, dusky dark, and the wall of glass gave the illusion that they were perched in the treetops like birds. Evelyn moved around the bed to go to the closet, but Jamie caught her hand. He didn't have to pull her, she moved toward him on her own, wanting his nearness, and she let him reach behind her to unzip the dress, his eyes on hers. She still had the pillow underneath. He slid the back open like pulling apart a snakeskin and pushed the sleeves down halfway, dropping the neckline below her breasts, her skin stippled with goosebumps from the cold. She could see the pink iridescence of his pupils in the gloaming as he touched her ribs—his hand was cold and she caught her breath, flinching, arms pinned by the sleeves of the dress. He watched her as he unbuttoned the cuffs of his sleeves, untied the silver bow tie under his chin, and slid off his cummerbund. When he opened his shirt, she pulled her arms out of the dress to touch the flossy, dark hair on his sternum. Her hands were cold too, and he winced.

They made love on the bed in their borrowed clothes. She straddled him and watched the galaxies in his eyes as he gripped her hips and the dress bunched around her—around the pillow inside it.

"Can I come inside you?" he asked, one hand on the fake belly.

She said yes and he did.

The last man she'd slept with was Packy, and theirs was an easy, drifting affection. Living in rooms across the hall from one another, there was never a question of whether someone would stay the night, whether he or she would go home, who had weekend plans, or whether they were seeing other people. She sneaked into his room and crawled into his bed. Sometimes he was waiting for her, sometimes he was asleep. They'd never even talked about birth control or condoms because Packy always pulled out.

Maybe that was why it was easy for him to disappear—they'd never been anything to one another, so he wasn't really leaving anything behind. She'd missed the lean, gristly toughness of his body, his boyish smile that showed all his squared-off, white teeth.

Jamie's body was different—softer in the backs of his arms, skinny legs. Packy's gristliness came from his work as a framer.

She and Packy had never had a rule about sleeping separately, but it had been rare for either of them to spend the night in the other's bed. When Erin left, their visits became less frequent. Mora—tiny, mewling—woke every two hours in those first months, and Evelyn could spend all night holding her with a bottle in hand. At first she tried sitting up in a kitchen chair she'd brought into her bedroom, pillow in her lap and Mora spread out on top of it with a bottle in her mouth, but she stopped doing that after she fell asleep and woke to the sound of Mora sliding off the pillow and hitting the ground. After that, she fed Mora in the bed.

She never even considered the possibility of asking Packy for help. Not even thinking of Packy. She hummed to stay awake. She sometimes hummed herself back to sleep and dreamed she was a wide, gleaming black piano and the two little girls were rolling to sleep across the strings inside her. No room for Packy in any of that—so maybe that's why it was easy for him to leave: she'd already left him behind.

She was thinking of Packy when she woke up the next morning in the wide, white bed to the shimmer of the bed frame leaves around them. In the gray light of morning, they were suspended in a mist—like the wrought iron vines were rising out of a thick fog in a silvery woodland.

She'd slept the whole night through.

She turned and saw Jamie behind her, asleep on his back with his arms folded over his bare chest.

The girls. Nan. She sat up in a breathless panic. She still had the dress around her middle—the pillow still inside.

"I gotta go home," she said, throwing off the white goose-down bedspread.

But Jamie's arm came around her waist and pulled her back. He rolled her underneath him, his back opening like wings that enfolded them as he pressed his erection against her, easily sliding back inside and crushing the pillow between them. His breath rushed in her ear like blood and it made her dizzy as her hair caught on his beard. She twisted onto her stomach as Jamie gripped her hips and pushed himself deeper into her.

They only became aware of the stinging cold when they were finished, panting and pink, tacky with sweat. Jamie pulled up the bedspread and they both rolled together underneath it. Evelyn felt the ooze of Jamie's semen between her legs, making her slippery. It was getting on the sheets.

She was aware of herself falling back to sleep. She was so tired—hadn't even realized how tired she was. How had she gone for so long on so little sleep? How did she get up and dress herself, drive her car an hour each way around the perimeter of the lake every day?

What day was it now?

Somewhere, she thought she heard Jamie's distant voice say, "Stay here." She felt his weight shift away from her, but she didn't open her eyes—sunk in the warmth of the bed and the humming of her bones.

When she woke, it was to the smell of food. Jamie was lying

next to her, but beside her head was a grilled cheese sandwich on a small glass plate. Orange-and-white cheese oozed out of the middle and Evelyn was starving. She grabbed the sandwich and ate it wolfishly. Jamie laughed.

"Slow down, monster."

Evelyn's fingers were greasy. Butter dripped from the bread and onto the sheets. As she took the last bite, she looked at the clock on the writing table. 12:17 p.m.

"Oh, God," she coughed, mouth full of food, as she sat up. "I'm late for work." She was on her knees, trying to untangle herself from the wadded sheets.

"You're not late. Your shift is over."

Evelyn froze, breath like a spray of sand in her throat. "Oh . . ." Where were her clothes?

"Don't go," said Jamie, his warm hand on her hip, pulling gently like a current.

"I can't lose my job. I'm so stupid." Evelyn pushed his hand away and finally disentangled herself. She stood up and the freezing air on her hot skin was like plunging into night water.

"I called in sick for you," said Jamie. "While you were sleeping."

Evelyn looked at him. "You did?"

Jamie smiled. "Of course. I said I was your husband and you were sick. I did it while I was downstairs making the sandwiches. Come back to bed."

Evelyn looked at him. He was smiling. He was lying. But what if he wasn't? What if he did call in for her? It was too late to go in now anyway.

She thought of Nan. Of Lila and Mora.

She shivered in the cold and Jamie reached out of the bed effortlessly, hooked an arm around her waist, and pulled her back to him. Before she could say anything—tell herself that she needed to go—his hand was moving between her slick thighs. He felt the thick ooze of his own spent semen and he moaned.

Jamie was talking to her, and she heard herself talking too.

"Uther," he said.

Her own voice said, "What?"

"That's what she's naming the baby."

"Oh."

"Uther. After Uther Pendragon. She said he was the father of King Arthur—as in, King Arthur and Camelot and the Round Table. All the kids at the country club have weird names. Wulf. Maebh. Johannes. There's even one named Prospero. Are you asleep?"

"Hmm?"

"Are you going back to sleep?"

"I'm listening," she hummed.

The sleep that she got with Jamie in the big, white, mist-shrouded bed was a death sleep, and every time she tried to move her arms and legs, to twist and rise, she sank deeper. She slept with her mouth open, unable to close it. Once, she woke up to Jamie kissing her ribs, stroking the flare of her hipbone and the sloping suspension of skin. She reached to touch his hair but felt something hard and pointed, and she opened her eyes to see deer antlers on his head, huge and heavy, sharp, branched like trees. She was afraid he'd gouge her eye. She tried to push them away, and Jamie caught her fingers in his mouth.

Later, she opened her eyes and he had boar tusks. She squeezed her eyes shut and opened them wide, trying to force herself awake, and she stared at the sharp, gleaming yellow tusks as he lifted his face from between her thighs and shape-shifted in front of her—something vulpine, something canine. An ungulate eater. Something forever hungry.

Sometimes the mist was so thick and dark that it looked like curtains around the bed. She dreamt about Lila and Mora—they were lost and growing sleepy in the misty glimmer. A night beast was stalking them with lathery haunches and dripping mouth.

When she woke, there was always food waiting for her—sandwiches, eggs, bacon, pan-seared scallops drizzled with a mushroom sauce, salmon baked with fresh dill and lemon, and once even steak—tender, blue inside, with a scoop of melting garlic-and-parsley butter on top so that steak juice dripped all over the sheets when she lifted the whole thing to her mouth. Jamie watched her eat, and when she finished, she went back to sleep.

She dreamed of the mountains, the trees. She was a little girl running through the woods in too-small clothes, pine cone petals in her hair, looking for wild blackberries with the other children as the sky darkened. They were running, trying to beat the rain and the creeping chill. Evelyn could hear Nan's piano music, which grew louder as she got closer to the little house at the edge of the woods. She ran faster as the tempo sped up, jumping over fallen trees soft with rot, landing in a patch of mud that sucked off her boots. She had to stop and fish them out with a long stick.

She put her muddy boots back on and turned to find herself face-to-face with Erin, who stood with her arms limp at her sides, loose tank top and orangey hair ruffling in the wind, staring back at Evelyn with dead, black eyes. Erin's face was gray and bony with grief, because she'd always known what Evelyn would do—had done.

Evelyn saw herself opening the front door again, saw Erin lying with her head and arms on the kitchen table, Moose and

Big Rob nodding off beside her in a crawling haze of blue smoke. Saw Lila standing naked and potbellied in the hallway, gripping her hands together and crying.

She saw Mora rolling in the overfilled bathtub.

Who had called Moose and Big Rob? Who told Moose that Erin was back—told him to come over and bring Big Rob because he was always good for pills?

Evelyn had called them. She knew Erin would get strung out—would leave again. Would leave the girls to Evelyn.

If she'd come home one minute later.

Every night, Mora was drowning in that bathtub and every night Evelyn and Lila were drowning with her. They'd ruptured the skin separating them from the darkness on the other side—the murky water wilds where the dead waited. Now they couldn't escape it. It followed them. And Evelyn was to blame.

Erin stood in front of her in the woods, the cavernous black of her eyes expanding, deepening, as she opened her mouth to speak, but no words came out. Just the volcanic groan of shifting ground.

When she woke up, there was a salad of wild greens in a large bowl on the bed—dandelion leaves, miner's lettuce, wild carrots, yellowfoot chanterelles. Wild blackberries. Had he gone outside and gathered all of it? But where would he have found dandelion greens and miner's lettuce in the snow? She lay back in the bed and closed her eyes and ate it with her fingers. Jamie brought a glass of water to her mouth.

Later, she felt him wiping her face with a warm, damp cloth. He dipped it in a bowl of water and she heard the streaming, dribbling patter as he wrung it out and wiped her neck, wiped the length of her arms, her hands—between her fingers, under her fingernails. He wiped the cloth down her armpits and along her chest, between and under her breasts. He wiped the damp cloth down her stomach, down her legs, wiped the arches of her feet, the skin between her toes, gently scrubbed the cuticles and beds of her toenails. He ran the cloth back up her thighs and wiped it carefully between her legs, smoothing a corner of the cloth between the labial folds. He dried her with another towel and then sat behind her head to brush out her hair, working through the knots and tangles with careful precision, never tugging. He rubbed her head with his fingers, scratched his fingernails along the back of her scalp to send a shimmering electric current down her spine. He cradled her jaw and rubbed his thumbs behind her ears and whispered something—another language. She couldn't understand it, couldn't even identify it because—she knew—it was prehistoric, and she felt tears sliding down her temples and into her hair.

Jamie went on rubbing the occipital bone above the nape of her neck—the bowl at the back of the skull that separates Homo sapiens from other hominins.

And somewhere deep inside herself, she imagined the lobe-finned beginnings of a baby. A spine leading up to the occipital bone of a bulbous skull—a spine the same S-shape as the cormorant's neck—the S-shape of the lake. A baby turning on its axis in her dark inner space.

Jamie kissed her on the forehead and said, "Time to go."

She opened her eyes. The windows were blazing white with the overcast sky, and the white room and white bed were blinding. She closed her eyes again and tried to go back to sleep.

"Nope," said Jamie, flipping the bedspread off of her. "Don't even try it."

The room was icy. She sucked in her breath.

"We can't stay," said Jamie.

When her eyes finally adjusted, Evelyn sat up. Her clothes were heaped at the foot of the bed where Jamie had thrown them.

"What day is it?" she asked, rubbing her face.

"Saturday."

Evelyn blinked, slow to translate. Three days. Strangely, though, she didn't feel the hot rush of panic. She dressed slowly, sluggishly. She looked at the mess of the bed and ached to get back in it with him, to be pressed into the mattress and buried alive. She looked at Jamie and saw that he was watching her, smiling as he buckled his belt.

"We can't stay?" she asked, wondering why she wasn't panicking.

Jamie laughed and shook his head. "The phone's been ringing all morning and I think someone's going to come to the house soon." He sat down in a chair to put on his socks but he kept his eyes on her, floating around her thighs. "We could come back."

Evelyn nodded, unsatisfied, as she pulled on her jeans and rolled her sports bra over her head. Jamie watched her dress, something like curiosity in the topography of his face.

They left the house together, descending the stairs and stepping out into the white morning light. Before they got into their separate cars, Jamie faced her with his hands on her shoulders. He stood a full head taller and he pressed his lips to her forehead, sighing into her hair. Evelyn closed her eyes and relaxed against him. Packy had never held her like that. No man had.

Jamie's hand slid under her shirt to graze the back of his

knuckles over her stomach—searing hot. And then he was kneeling and holding the cradle of her hips, pressing his ear to her abdomen, still and unmoving, like he was listening for something. Something ancient—something fantastic blooming inside her.

NAN

Nan couldn't be angry with Evelyn. She'd been gone for three days, no calls home, not answering her phone, just like the time before when she left in the night without a goodbye, without a note or a phone call. Back then it had taken Evelyn two months to finally send Nan a postcard letting her know she was okay. Nan had always known better than to ask her where she was—or to ask her to come home. She'd always known that chasing Evelyn was like trying to catch strands of oil in water.

So when Jube ate her cereal at the kitchen counter in dribbling spoonfuls and asked with her dripping mouth, "The hell did she go?" Nan had to pretend she knew. Didn't want Jube thinking Nan didn't know Evelyn.

"Visiting a friend. She told me she'd be gone for a few days." And Nan had hoped she was right. Evelyn couldn't stay away from the girls. If she'd left for good, she would've taken them with her.

The thought of Evelyn leaving made her itch, made her scratch at the hot spot on her neck until it flaked and went sticky. The rash had become a constellation of tiny, pink-white bumps under her jawbone.

When Evelyn walked back through the front door with a fresh-scrubbed glow of heat and contentment, Nan just smiled and squeezed her hand and said, "Want some coffee?"

"I'm okay, thanks," Evelyn said, kissing Nan on the cheek. She smelled different—like the nitrogen cut of black earth. "Where are my babies at?"

Evelyn got down on the living room floor with Lila and Mora, who screamed as they climbed on her and knocked their skulls into her nose and forehead. Mora grabbed her by the ears and hair and chewed on her chin. Lila wheezed into a coughing fit. Evelyn brought her a sippy cup of water and then went to her bedroom to call work. Nan listened, heard her voice through the door. "I know . . . I'm sorry, Bobby . . ."

Jube spent the afternoon in her room with her yapping dogs. She'd brought with her a tiny TV with a built-in VCR, along with a stack of old VHS tapes, and Nan could hear it blaring almost constantly. Sometimes she watched animal shows that the dogs barked at. At night, the blue light flickered under Jube's door but no sound came from the room, which meant Jube had muted the TV.

Nan started making dinner, and when the smell of onions sweating in butter had filled the house, Jube came out of her room. She drifted into the kitchen and leaned a hip against the counter as she watched Nan chop up mushrooms and fresh thyme and add them to the pan. When Nan poured in a splash of white wine, Jube groaned.

"Chicken tetrazzini? Again?"

Nan slammed the bottle down harder than she'd meant to, making Rosie jump awake on the couch. "What do you mean, 'chicken tetrazzini again'? I don't see you making dinner."

"You already made it twice in the last week. Nobody eats that much chicken tetrazzini!"

"Lila needs to gain weight," Nan snapped, trying not to wave her butcher knife as she spoke. She cleared her throat, took a breath—the way she used to when she taught at the high school. "Lila needs to gain weight and the best way to do that is through starches and fats—which means pasta and cream sauce."

Jube puffed out a mocking laugh. "She'll gain weight all right. At this rate, we'll all be too big to get in an elevator together."

Nan slammed the knife down. "If you're not going to help then get the hell out of my kitchen."

"It ain't *your* kitchen if it's *my* kid payin the bills around here."

Nan clucked in disbelief, but before she could say anything in response, Jube had tossed her frizzled hair over her shoulder and gone back to her room.

"You do make a lot of chicken tetrazzini," said Clara as she walked hunchbacked out of the same hallway that Jube had just stormed into. She was rubbing her dry palms together as if working the dust from them.

"The nerve she has to come into my house and criticize my cooking," said Nan as she laid out four chicken breasts in the pan of onions to cook.

"*Your* house?" Clara said.

Nan stirred the chicken and onions and then clacked the wooden spoon against the pan. "Don't start."

Clara lowered herself stiffly to a kitchen chair. "At least she's here to help you keep an eye on Evelyn."

"How's that?"

"Girl's gotten in over her head."

"What are you talking about?"

Clara looked at Nan pointedly. "She's after a man."

"You think I don't know that?"

"She's gonna get distracted—she'll get sloppy. She's got to stay focused on them girls," said Clara, leaning an elbow on the back of the chair and looking at Nan grimly. "She can't let em get away from her."

Nan frowned. "What on earth does that mean?"

The chicken popped in the butter and Nan flinched. Clara was gone.

"Nan? Who are you talking to?" asked Evelyn. She had come into the kitchen quietly, Mora on her hip, and she was frowning at Nan.

Nan sighed. "No one. Don't worry about it."

She went on making dinner, pretending not to notice the concern lining Evelyn's mouth as she went back to the living room, periodically glancing at Nan.

Nan boiled the linguine, strained it, and dumped it in a buttered casserole dish. She stirred in the diced chicken and onions, the cream sauce, some boiled peas, and some Parmesan cheese, and then baked the whole thing in the oven. When it was browned on the top, she yelled, "Dinner's ready!" and took the dish out of the oven, setting it on a potholder on the table. Evelyn came in and put Mora in the high chair, grabbing the box of Cheerios off the top of the fridge and shaking some out on the tray to keep Mora busy so she could set the table.

Jube drifted in and sat down at the table while Nan filled glasses of water for everyone and Evelyn cut up noodles and chicken for the girls.

"It's gonna be chicken tetrazzini leftovers for the rest of the week," Jube sighed.

Nan slapped a spoonful of casserole on Jube's plate.

Jube smirked as Nan and Evelyn clasped their hands under their chins for the dinner blessing.

"Bless us, O Lord, and these thy gifts, which we're about

to receive, from thy bounty, through Christ our Lord," said Nan. "Amen."

They ate in silence. Jube used the edge of her fork to pick the peas out of her linguine and push them over to one side.

"If the slop weren't bad enough, there has to be peas in it too," Jube grumbled. She looked up at Nan to see her reaction.

"You can make dinner next time then."

"You really want to let me make dinner or are you just sayin what you think will put me in my place?" asked Jube as she twisted linguine on her fork. "Because if you mean it, I'll make dinner tomorrow night. Frozen burritos and tater tots like you wouldn't believe."

"Stop it," said Evelyn.

Nan sighed, went back to eating her food, tried not to hear Jube's loud, smacking eating sounds.

"If that's what will make you happy, Jubilee Rae—sure," Nan finally said. "Make burritos and tater tots. It would be a nice change." She knew that Jube was angling for a fight, another kitchen floor brawl. But she also couldn't ignore the guilt that swam in the dark water of her thoughts: had she taken Evelyn? Had she taken something from Jube?

Jube went on eating, but Nan could feel her stare and looked up to find Jube smiling at her as she chewed.

"You still talk to me like we're back in your high school science class," she said, pointing the tines of her fork at Nan. "Actin like you were there to save us—to help us degenerates."

"Be quiet," Evelyn said.

Jube held up her hands defensively. "Honest to God. She acted so patient, so loving—like she just wanted to help all us lowlifes!" Jube laughed. "How do I get through to these hicks?" Balling her fists under her chin and pleading up at the ceiling.

"Enough, Jube!" Evelyn yelled. Lila started crying, bending

her head over her plate so that her hair dragged through the cream sauce. Evelyn stroked her cheek and rubbed the back of her neck. "Don't cry. I'm sorry."

"Huh. Losing your temper and making your babies cry. Shameful," Jube grumbled. "Still the same old Evie."

Nan stood up. "You be quiet or you can get out of my house right now."

Jube slammed her fork down and stood up too. "You gonna make me? You gonna call the cops? Be my guest." She looked at Evelyn. "Because I'm sure that's what you want to do when you're holdin onto someone else's kids and pretending they're your own."

Her words left a ringing in the air and Nan and Evelyn stared in wordless panic.

"You really think you can pass em off as yours?" said Jube. "Look at em. I bet their real mama is white enough to see through."

Nan looked at Lila, at Mora, both with big, sad well-water eyes and round faces. Not Evelyn's eyes. Not her bones.

Nan sat back down, and Jube finally lowered herself to her chair as well. The women sat in silence while Mora slapped her hand on her tray, smashing the peas.

Jube looked at Evelyn with something like motherly firmness in her face, like she'd decided on something. "I ain't plannin on telling. If you took those girls, it was for a good reason. But let's be real. If their mama didn't give em to you . . ." She tilted her head forward slightly, raised her eyebrows. "Then she's lookin for em. Or she got people lookin for em. Was it drugs?"

Evelyn nodded silently.

"Then she won't call the police. Did you ever mention where you were from?" asked Jube.

Nan wondered why she hadn't thought to ask these questions.

"I don't know," Evelyn finally said, shaking her head. "I might've. I can't remember."

"You need to remember," Jube said firmly. "Because if you did, you can't stay in Cormorant Lake."

Nan hadn't considered the possibility of Evelyn leaving—leaving and taking the two little girls with her. An empty house again.

Nan sat on the side of the bed, lamp off so she wouldn't draw Evelyn's attention. She had always known, of course, that Evelyn and the girls couldn't stay—that it wasn't safe—but it was too painful to admit. After so many years alone with only Clara to talk to, how could she watch them leave?

"She's listening, you know," said Clara, who was sitting on the hope chest at the end of the bed. She'd taken off her shoes and was rubbing her bad foot. Dust was drizzling from it in the moonlight. She waved a hand at the door. "She hears you movin around in here and she's listening."

"Then keep your voice down," Nan whispered. Evelyn was getting ready for her night shift at the gas station. She hadn't bothered trying to sleep beforehand.

"You knew they couldn't stay forever," said Clara. "You can't have what ain't yours."

"But if they go . . ." Nan's throat was too tight to draw breath. She scratched at her neck, felt scabs open and ooze. Blood under her fingernails. "I couldn't bear it." She squeezed her hands together to keep from crying. "Everyone has left me. First Earl, then you and Peter." She didn't say the surgeon's name, even though they both knew she was thinking it. "And then Evelyn came along and I had her. She was mine."

She went clear-eyed, thinking back to the nights she'd made

dinner for the two of them, shaving the precious truffles thin and layering them on top of a bowl of noodles so that they glistened. The nights she sat grading at the kitchen table while Evelyn did her homework beside her, the way Evelyn bent her head over her notebook so her hair fell and the bony ridge stood out on the back of her neck and Nan had to touch it.

"If she leaves again—I just couldn't bear it," she whispered to Clara, who was listening quietly, grimly, not meeting Nan's eyes. "I can't bear it."

Someone moved in the hallway. Nan went silent and listened, watching the shadow under the door.

"He's down there," Clara whispered, rising. Her shoes were back on her feet. "Peter. He loved you. He's there waiting for you."

The listener in the hallway shifted on her feet, and a floorboard squeaked.

"I'll take you to him."

Nan gestured impatiently to the door. How would they get past the listener on the other side?

"This way," said Clara. Nan twisted around and saw that Clara was outside now, standing beneath the snowy cedars.

Nan put on her robe, jacket, and boots and opened the window. The screen came out with a pop, and she pulled her chair under the window and stepped up. First one leg out, lowering her foot carefully down to the water meter, which was sheeted in ice.

"Easy now, old girl," said Clara. "Nice and easy."

Then the other leg—but Nan's foot slipped off the water meter and she slid sideways, grabbing onto the side of the window frame with both hands as her feet hit the ground hard.

"Good Lord . . ." said Clara.

"I've never done this before!"

"I think the whole damn town knows that now."

Nan winced, rubbing the sore spot on her ribcage where she'd hit the windowsill.

"Come on," said Clara, who was already standing in the middle of the road, hair gleaming blue in the moonlight.

"I'm coming," Nan said as she shuffled stiffly after Clara.

By the time she reached the muddy street, Clara was calling her from the bottom of the hill, standing there in the snow with her thin shoulders rolled forward.

"Come on, you old bitty," she called. "Hitch up your bloomers and keep up."

Nan huffed after her, careful to step sideways so she wouldn't go sliding down the hill, breath puffing in the night air as she felt her nose run and her lips go numb. She didn't so much follow Clara as chase after her, trying to catch up as Clara appeared at the edge of Linden Lane, on the other side of the gate, at the top of the hill, on the other side of the flooded dip in the road, and around the bend of rhododendrons. Finally, she stood just beyond the ruins of the old house, at the edge of the cliff that overlooked the wide, black lake, skirt snapping in the wind like the starlit figurehead on the prow of a ship.

Nan edged around the old house, hearing the skitter and squeak of mice inside. Something huge soared out of the roof—an arcing haze against the night sky—an owl. She came to stand beside Clara and looked down at the water below, little more than a moldering, wooden handrail acting as the line between them and a two-hundred-foot drop. The white mountains rose straight out of the water, and the glassy surface mirrored their slopes so the lake looked like a starry underworld. An inverted night.

They stood facing north. To the right: the eastern mountain slope where the train derailed and went crashing through the trees and earth to disappear in the water.

"He's down there," said Clara. "Our boy."

Nan looked at the still, dark water below. Somewhere within that inverted night was a distant sparking nucleus.

"Is it very deep?" Nan asked. "Is it cold?" She put her hand on Clara's shoulder, sending up a cloud of dust.

Clara was nodding her head slowly, chewing the corner of her mouth. "It's very deep. It's very cold," she said. "I won't lie to you."

"Does he know I'm here? Can he see me?" Her breath was thin, throat tight. "Is he close?"

Clara was looking at her, frowning through the darkness.

"You remember what the judge said to me?" Clara asked.

Nan blinked, forcing herself to focus through the tears.

"When I tried to get him back. When I took Linden to court. You remember what the judge said to me?"

Nan couldn't think. She closed her eyes, tried to remember, but when she opened her eyes, she was staring down at the water, at the soaring depths. On the water's surface, she could see the owl that had flown out of the house cutting across the night sky—two owls soaring across the lake in parallel formation to meet at a point on the other side. If she stared at the water long enough, she would forget which night was the real one. She could tip forward, let go of the ground, and fall into the sky.

"He said, 'The court sympathizes with Miss Lark, but believes that it would be cruel to remove the boy from his home with Doctor Bradford Linden, who has been his primary caregiver these last five months, and to whom the child has no doubt formed an affectionate attachment.'" She was speaking as if reading from a transcript, and she enunciated "affectionate attachment" with hard, spitting *t*'s. "We believe that given Peter's extensive medical needs, which will require numerous corrective surgeries, Doctor Bradford Linden will have more knowledge and foresight to ensure Peter receives the care he needs. Further, we have reservations about returning a vulnerable child to a chronically absent, unmarried mother." Upper lip curling back from her teeth—something like disgust. "While he was putting my boy on display like some circus freak. The Boy Without a Face," she spat. Her eyes sparked hot in the darkness. "No one in this town stood up for me. No one. Not Myrna or Helen, not Linney, not Mary." She turned on Nan. "Where were you?"

Nan felt her hands fly apart. "Me?"

"You didn't stand up for me." Clara looked out at the water and frowned. "You were in love with him. The man who stole my boy."

They both settled into a lake-bottom silence. Clara looked down at the water.

"He's waiting for us," she said, looking at Nan.

Nan blinked and Clara was gone. She looked down, and there was Clara in the water, looking up at her from just below the surface, floating in the glittery dark. An invitation. The wind fluttered Nan's robe and she shivered, wondering how cold the water was.

A hand snatched her back from the cliff's edge, a gruff voice whispering, "What the fuck?" She was whipped around face-to-face with Jube, lips rolled tight in furious alarm.

"What are you doin out here?" Jube said. "Crazy . . ." She shook her head as she pulled Nan away from the cliff, away from the house, back down the road.

Nan woke up in her bed. Her room was bright with sunlight—a clear sky, a high sun, trees already slanting their shadows. Her robe was hanging where she left it on the door. Her boots were in her closet. Had she slept? Had she left the house last night?

She got out of bed and stepped into her slippers, zipped up her robe, and padded out of her room. Morning sunlight blazed on the walls. Outside, she could see the frosty grass smoking. In the kitchen, Mora was in her high chair, slapping her hands on the tray and bellowing.

"All right, all right, I'm going as fast as I can," Evelyn said as she hurried to the high chair with a box of Cheerios. Mora grabbed fistfuls of Cheerios and crammed them into her gumming, wet mouth.

Lila was eating cheesy eggs—always like she hadn't eaten in months. Evelyn was still buttering the toast as she set it on Lila's plate, but Lila's thin hand shot out, grabbed it, and shoved it in her mouth.

Jube was scraping scrambled eggs off the pan and onto three large plates. She looked up when Nan stepped into the kitchen. She didn't say anything.

"Hey," Evelyn said, eyebrows raised. "Where were you?"

Nan stopped.

"I thought I heard you leave the house last night." Evelyn added, "You feeling okay?"

"Of course I'm feeling okay," said Nan as she got the cream out of the fridge and poured it into a mug.

"You never sleep in," said Evelyn. "I was about to check on you. Did you have trouble sleeping?" Evelyn narrowed her eyes, scrutinizing. "You don't look right."

Nan clucked. "What a thing to say to someone."

"You look—I don't know. Tired."

"Well I just woke up, didn't I?" Nan poured coffee into the cream. "And you're one to talk."

Evelyn smiled. "Come eat."

Jube and Evelyn brought the plates to the table—eggs and toast and microwaved precooked sausage. That must have been

Jube's idea. Nan sat down with them and tried not to wrinkle her nose at the rubbery meat. She quickly rolled one of the sausages onto the floor for Rosie and saw Jube glance sideways at her. Nan realized a moment later that Jube was also sneaking sausages into her napkin and rolling them up under her plate to take back to her dogs.

They ate quietly together, and then Evelyn set her fork down.

"I lost my job at the country club," she said, and looked at Nan, weariness edging into her face for the first time since she disappeared for three days.

Nan understood her meaning: the country club was one of the only places in Cormorant Lake where someone could find a steady job. If Evelyn had been fired, she couldn't hope to work at the country club again.

"Can you find some more truffles? Just to keep us above water until I can find another job?" Evelyn asked.

"We're not *underwater*," Nan said. "But yes, I can always find more truffles."

She pretended not to see Jube watching her.

She could hear Jube behind her somewhere as she walked carefully through the icy ferns. She walked with her hands out, touching the mossy tree trunks, the pine boughs that shook water in her face. Her hands were slimed in algae.

Jube was following her but she didn't know how to step lightly. She stomped dead pine needles, kicked through hard snow, and plowed rocks out of her way, but whenever Nan looked back, Jube was nowhere to be seen.

Nan kept walking, following the rich, earthy truffle scent. They were near.

Clara's words were ringing in her head like the gong of the church bell. *Where were you?*

She heard the crash of a rock rolling downhill and splashing into a stream behind her.

"Stop following me, Jube, I'm trying to think!" Nan yelled.

She paused, waited for the truffle current to find her again. She turned left, sidestepped down the ravine to the spot at the bottom where the scent was strongest. She lowered herself painfully to her knees on a patch of icy soil at the base of a snowy, blue Douglas fir and started digging with her trowel.

Where were you?

She sat back on her heels. "I was living in your mother's house with you," she said, baffled. "I was right there the whole time. You were trying to get him back and the judge ruled against you—I was right there in the courtroom with you."

The woods were silent. An arctic wind swirled up the back of her neck and chilled her to her gut.

"Clara," she called. "I was right there."

No answer. Clara was nowhere.

Nan shook her head at Clara's stubbornness as she went on digging, feeling the fleshy give of the truffles underneath. But rather than the familiar spongy knot, the lump was larger, wider. She carefully brushed the soil with her fingers so she wouldn't rupture it.

Where were you?

Nan had tried to get Peter back in the months after she gave him to the surgeon, before Clara returned, but the sheriff told her that it wasn't a kidnapping if she wasn't the child's legal parent or guardian. What was she to Peter? She was no mother.

There had been other people in the courtroom, people who didn't want to take a side, who liked the surgeon and thought he was doing great things for the town—it was *his* money that had built the library, the school playground—but were also ill at ease with the idea of a judge telling a mother she could not have her child back.

Myrna had been there. And Helen, and Linney. Even Mary.

Myrna and Terry had both taken the stand to testify on behalf of the surgeon.

"He paid me to reroof his house," Terry had said. "He was polite and courteous and paid me on time. He never tried to talk me down on the price and even tipped me an extra hundred dollars when it was done. The boy was running around playing when I was there. Looked perfectly happy to me."

"He paid for the new baptismal font at the church and a statue of the Blessed Virgin in the courtyard," Myrna had said. "I believe he's a good man and if he thinks that Peter would be better off with him, then he must have a good reason." She stood up to leave, but then hesitated, added, "I'm sorry but no true mother could bear to leave her child like that."

Had Nan said anything to Myrna after that? Had Nan even disagreed with her? Or had she secretly thought, *Yes, no true mother.*

Her fingers brushed the dirt away from a pale mound. It was moving, a slight undulation, and she snatched her hands back. The mound went still.

Where was she?

She had been there when Linden shook his lawyer's hand, triumphant, smiling, shaking hands with the people gathered around them. She had been there when Clara turned to her, bloodless, lips shrank back from her teeth like a corpse. Dazed.

She had driven Clara home in the pickup truck Clara's father had left behind when he died—and then her mother left behind when she died. It wasn't until they got home that Clara turned to Nan and said, "They took my child from me."

Nan dug around the mound, carved into the mud with her

fingers and pulled out dirt clods—the mound started moving again. There was a bony protrusion. She scooped away the frozen earth and saw a tiny, mouse-frail ribcage. She kept digging. Tiny arms. She swept the earth away from a tiny face—a baby—dirt in its nose and eyes. It opened its wet mouth and took a breath, and Nan fell backward.

The baby was gone.

She was staring at an empty hole in the ground.

She felt a hand on her shoulder and looked up to find Jube kneeling over her.

"The baby. Did you see it?" Nan asked.

Jube looked at the hole in the ground, then down at Nan's muddy hands, bleeding where her fingernails had torn.

"Come on. We gotta get you home," said Jube, moving behind Nan and heaving her up by her armpits.

But Nan yanked her arms away.

"Where did the baby go?" Nan demanded, feeling her eyes grow hot with tears.

"They always go," Jube said. "The babies never stay."

Nan waved her hands in annoyance. "That's not what I mean. I mean the baby—the one that was right there."

"You know why my mom left me?" said Jube. "She came to me in a dream right after I had Evelyn. She said she left because she thought I'd be her baby, but I wasn't. She said as soon as I was born, she saw the yellow tint of my hair and my dad's nose and knew I was his baby, not hers. She took care of me because I needed takin care of, but she said I'd never be hers." She sighed through her nose, which came out as a steamy puff. "She was wrong. I deserve a mother just like everyone else."

Nan looked back at the hole in the ground, wondering who had left the baby behind.

"Come on, it's fuckin cold," said Jube, pulling Nan away.

EVELYN

When Evelyn called the country club and said she'd been sick, Tanya said, "They've hired a new deckhand," and hung up. Bobby at the gas station was more forgiving. "People have emergencies but you got to have someone call—it's called responsibility," he lectured. She went to her night shift on Monday, and when she left Tuesday morning, she bought a full tank of gas and drove an hour to the north shore, not knowing if Jamie would be at Ursula's house. But there was his car in the driveway. The front door was unlocked.

She found him in the bedroom, sitting in an armchair by the floor-to-ceiling windows with one leg draped lazily over the arm as he gazed out at the lake below—not quite a part of the space around him, but trying to claim it anyway. A large, white egret swooped past the glass, barely visible in the mist. When Evelyn stopped beside him, Jamie looked at her with a bright smile, and in the blaze of white light, she saw how young he was.

He swung his leg off the chair and took her hips in his hands, pressing his forehead into her stomach. She ran her hands through his hair and looked out the window. The mist was moving, crawling, and as it cleared in gaps, she could see the lake. Loons and cormorants were sliding through the water, dipping and diving. She thought she could see something swell up in the water and crest, but it didn't break the surface before disappearing again into the bottomless deep.

She looked around the room and realized it had been cleaned, sheets washed, bed made. The plush white carpet had been vacuumed—overlapping tracks crossing from one wall to the other.

As if sensing her confusion, Jamie lifted his head and said, "The housekeepers." His stomach growled loudly and he leaned back in the chair and stretched his arms. "Are you hungry?"

He was smiling at her, eyes large and clear, childlike in their round searching openness.

"I can't stay," she said.

Jamie sat upright, hands dropping to his thighs.

"You're leaving?" he asked. "You just got here."

"I lost my job," said Evelyn. "The country club fired me."

"I'll help you get a new one. Abby's been looking for a nanny since she had the baby."

"Abby?"

"She was my—" Jamie stopped.

"Your girlfriend? One of your girlfriends?" Evelyn asked.

Jamie sat at the edge of the armchair. He was looking at her, waiting for her to say more.

"You, what? Still keep in touch?" Evelyn asked.

"We're friends," Jamie said, like a student answering a teacher's question.

Evelyn felt her blood pump faster, even though she'd already known there were other women—even though they were standing in his lover's bedroom. "How many have there been?"

"Three," Jamie said. "Abby, Sarah, Ursula."

"All at the same time?"

Jamie frowned. "No, never. I don't cheat."

"All pregnant?"

"Yes."

"What happens when they have the baby?"

Jamie rubbed the back of his head. "Then it doesn't work anymore."

They both fell silent. Jamie didn't raise his eyes to hers—mournful. Something about his grief made her stomach contract, and she stepped away from him.

He took her hand. "Don't go," he said. "Please." His eyes were wide and glittering in the window light.

And then his face opened up in a dazzling smile—the bright, milk teeth smile a boy turns on his mother. The smile she'd seen him turn on his pregnant lover.

When she didn't move away, he pulled her to him, unbuttoned her jeans, and opened them just wide enough to kiss the pale skin between the cliffs of her hip bones. He exhaled and she felt his warm, light breath on her stomach as he said, "What if?" He didn't finish the question.

He pressed his ear to her belly.

She knew that he was imagining the same thing she was: a mass of cells dividing and multiplying with impossible speed, turning into something more—a spine uncurling somewhere inside her deep, moonless dark.

When she left the house, the mist was heavy in the northern mountains and it enveloped the car so that when she looked out her window she could barely make out the front door, even though it was only a few yards away. She drove carefully up the driveway, straining to see through the blue fog that left everything gauzy and undefined.

As she drove back toward the south shore, the mist gradually cleared from the road and trees, but it still crawled in curling plumes along the surface of the lake. Something in the water moved, sliding greasy—a snaking tendril—leaving behind a gentle lapping wave before it disappeared.

She parked in the gravel driveway and saw that Jube's car was gone.

When she went inside, the TV was on and Mora was slumped over asleep in her high chair, spaghetti sauce smeared across her cheeks and hair in a dried, hardened glaze. Lila was asleep on the couch.

"Nan," Evelyn called as she quickly pulled Mora out of the high chair and took her to the sink to wipe her face.

Mora woke up with a hoarse whimper when Evelyn began cleaning her face with a wet washcloth. Snot was dried on her upper lip and Evelyn had to pull the washcloth tight over her finger and scrub hard.

"Nan," she called again.

Once she'd gotten Mora's face clean, she took her into the bedroom and got a clean shirt, since her pink *Beauty and the Beast* sweater was crusted over in sauce and dried noodles. Evelyn sat down on the bed with Mora in her lap and got her changed, then she hefted her onto her hip and carried her to Nan's room, which was empty. She went to the window and looked out at the backyard but couldn't see Nan anywhere.

She was striding quickly out of the bedroom when the front door opened and Nan came in with her basket, her boots and pants caked in mud. Her hair was frizzy and tangled with twigs and leaves. A clump of earth dangled from a strand of hair at her temple.

"Where were you?" Evelyn barked. "How long have you been gone?"

Nan blinked, stunned. "I've been out finding truffles like you asked. I found about eight hundred dollars' worth."

"Where's Jube?"

"How should I know?"

Evelyn reached for the wall to steady herself. "Who was watching the girls? How long've they been here by themselves?"

Nan frowned. "You're here with them. I thought you were watching them."

Outside the front window, Jube's headlights swung off the road and into the gravel driveway beside Evelyn's car. Even from inside, Evelyn could see Jube's Chihuahuas jumping around the back seat. They tumbled out with her and bounced like springs, yapping as she went to the trunk and got out two full plastic grocery bags and a pot of geraniums, yipping and bouncing as they followed her up the porch steps.

Evelyn opened the front door before Jube could even reach for the knob.

"Where were you?" she blasted.

Jube tucked her chin the same way Nan did when she was offended. "I was getting groceries." Holding up the geraniums. "What? You're not my mother. I'm the mother—"

"How long were Lila and Mora alone in the house?" Evelyn shouted.

Jube blinked. "Alone? Nan was here when I left. What do you mean they were alone?"

Evelyn shook her head and carried Mora to the living room. Over the back of the couch, she could see Lila's blue-veined bare feet sticking out, one ankle crossed over the other. But when Evelyn moved to the other side, Lila's face was driftwood white and her lips were blue. She had her fingers in her mouth but her lips were slack.

"Lila," Evelyn said, dropping Mora on the couch and grabbing Lila by the armpits. "Lila, honey."

But Lila's head flopped loosely. Evelyn heard herself saying "Lila, Lila," as she touched the little girl's mouth to feel for her breath. It was shallow, coming in short rasps. Evelyn put her ear to Lila's chest and listened to the tight rattling inside.

She didn't say anything to Jube and Nan as she wrapped Lila in the afghan and carried her and Mora, one on each hip, out to the car.

The hospital was midway between the north and south shores, just off the highway, and Evelyn halved the normal drive time so that she was there in fifteen minutes—almost losing Nan and Jube, who followed in Jube's car, hugging the tight curves and turns along with Evelyn so they never trailed more than a few car lengths behind.

Evelyn carried both girls into the emergency room and checked in at the front window. She sat down and Jube and Nan hurried inside from the parking lot. Nan murmured something to Jube and they both sat on the other side of the waiting room.

When the nurse called her in, Nan and Jube rose to follow but Evelyn looked at them with a set jaw, and they both sank back into their seats.

The doctor—older, red nosed, large pores—measured Lila's oxygen levels with a monitor he clipped to her tiny, blue-tipped finger. Her results came back: 84 percent.

"Anything below ninety is cause for concern," the doctor said, peering into Lila's throat, nose, and ears, listening to her tight breathing with his stethoscope. "She's having trouble fighting the infection," he added.

"She seemed to be getting better," said Evelyn, hitching

Mora up on her hip as the baby reached for the light switch behind her.

The doctor removed the earbuds of his stethoscope. "It could be immunosuppression, owing to her low weight. Was she was born prematurely?"

Evelyn shook her head, eyes closed, trying to recall words. "I don't . . ."

The doctor prescribed amoxicillin.

As Evelyn drove the mountain roads home, she looked in the rearview mirror at Lila. Head tipped back and neck arched birdlike, mouth open. Her tongue twitched slightly over her teeth. When they got home, Evelyn lifted the little girl out of her seat carefully. Lila laid her head heavily on Evelyn's shoulder and her goaty legs dangled.

By the time Evelyn had made macaroni and cheese for Mora and given Lila her medicine and breathing treatment, it was seven thirty and Mora's head was listing in her high chair. Evelyn wiped the baby's face and hands with a warm washcloth and carried her into the bedroom, where Lila was already curled up in bed. She changed both girls into nighttime diapers because Lila had been wetting the bed lately, and then wriggled Mora into one of Evelyn's clean T-shirts before tucking them in together.

She went out to the kitchen, where Jube and Nan were eating dinner quietly. Her two mothers.

"I gotta go to work in a couple of hours. No one leaves the house tonight," she said.

Nan set down her fork and straightened her spine. "I have no plans to leave."

"I came home and no one was here with the girls. Mora looked like she'd been stuck in her high chair for hours and Lila was barely breathing." Evelyn cleared her throat to try to keep from raising her voice.

Jube held up her hands, palms out, as she scooted her chair back from the table. "Don't look at me. Nan was here with them when I left."

"Well I didn't just walk out the door and leave them here alone," Nan scoffed.

"Do you remember leaving the house?" Evelyn asked.

Nan thought. She frowned. "Well. I know I didn't leave them here alone."

Evelyn's eyes met Jube's, and she could see that she knew something about Nan.

"Just. Don't leave tonight," Evelyn said to both of them before going back to the bedroom.

She tried to sleep but couldn't, lying awake and listening to Lila's shallow breathing. Mora rolled over and farted in her sleep. At nine thirty, Evelyn went out to get her boots. Nan and Jube were asleep in their rooms. Evelyn stopped in the hallway. She could hear the creak of Nan's bedsprings and she thought about knocking, asking, "Are you awake?" the way she did when she was a teenager. But she didn't.

She stuck her phone, wallet, and keys in her pockets and left, driving through the dark slowly so she wouldn't skid across black ice. The night was a watertight dark—she'd forgotten what real night looked like after she moved to California—and she didn't come to a light until she stopped at Main Street, under the traffic signal that hung suspended on a wire across the intersection. She waited, and then a car rolled through the intersection: an old, red Nissan covered in cumulus splotches of peeling clear coat, windows down because they were probably busted. Heading east to her north. As it crossed her headlights, she saw the flash of dry, broom-straw-red hair, the white scoop of jawbone. Erin. She blinked. The woman was gone, the car was rolling away, taillights a dry bleed in the fog.

She drove on, checking her mirrors for the car—wondering if it would turn around and come after her. But it was gone, and she realized she'd only been sleeping in small catches of hours and minutes.

She parked her car at the gas station and got out, but as she approached the doors, she saw a man leaning against the wall out front. She recognized him by his rangy leanness, the hunch of his shoulders, and she stopped. A cigarette was glowing between his fingers, and in the light of the convenience store, she could see his breath puffing out in the cold. Packy smiled at her.

"I knew if I was going to catch you before your shift, I'd have to get here at least fifteen minutes early because you're always early," he said, lifting himself off the wall and rubbing his right arm with his left so that the glowing cigarette was a blur of light.

Evelyn stared. Even in the dark she could see that he was still beautiful in that raggedy, orphaned way of his, but the fact that he'd found her left a coil of dread in her gut.

"I went back to the house looking for you," he said.

And because she didn't know what else to say, she said, "You can't smoke within a hundred feet of the gas pumps."

Packy looked down at his cigarette as if just realizing it was there. He stubbed it out on the wall and then dropped it on the ground, but then his hands were flighty. He never knew what to do with them—which, Evelyn had always assumed, was why he smoked so much.

"I went back to the house," he said again.

Evelyn didn't move, breath held because she didn't want him to see her panting, didn't want the fog to cloud her view of him. When he scratched the back of his neck and didn't say anything more, Evelyn said, "Was Erin there?"

"No one was there. Except Doris Clearwater. She said you

left with those two little girls." He looked at her and his hands went still. "They all know what you did."

Evelyn's throat closed. She was still holding her car keys and she fought the urge to get back in her car and drive home, to grab Lila and Mora and drive away from Cormorant Lake forever. "Does anyone know I'm here?"

Packy laughed a joyless laugh. "Evelyn, no one in that house even knew your last name. Not even Doris. I remembered you saying something about your family in Cormorant Lake and I came here to find you—which wasn't hard. There's one gas station in the whole town," he said, waving his hand up at the gas station sign.

Evelyn looked up at the sign, the *E* in Guthrie flickering, and she thought of the time Packy gave her a metal rose that he'd welded at a job site. The petals had gleamed smooth and bright, curving slightly like tongues, and the stem was stippled with three sharp steel thorns. On the underside of the rose's hips, a single, gleaming letter *E* that had been cut into the metal.

"I gotta clock in," she said. "You should go, Packy."

Packy didn't say anything as she walked past him and went inside. Lindy was at the counter, fresh-faced with her blue eye shadow and cream foundation despite the late hour.

"You see that guy lurking like a creep?" she said.

Evelyn went to the office to clock in, and by the time she came out to open her register, Packy was gone.

But when her shift was over at six the next morning, he was waiting outside in the predawn darkness, shoulders hunched in his hoodie and hands in the kangaroo pocket. It was always coldest right before dawn, colder now than it had been when she'd started her shift, and Packy had been up all night. She could tell by the waxy pallor in his cheeks—exhaustion. Still, she tried not to laugh at the fact that he thought a hoodie would be any good against a Cormorant Lake winter.

Evelyn unlocked her car and gestured for Packy to get in. They both slid into the seats and Packy made a gruffling sound and rubbed his arms as Evelyn started the car. She didn't turn the heater on right away since it would only blow cold air, and Packy looked at her expectantly—impatiently.

"Give it a minute," she said.

They were both silent as they waited for the engine to warm up. Packy's knee joggled and he tucked his hands between his thighs to warm them. He smelled like a shop: hot metal, fresh-cut wood, a faint afterthought of diesel fumes. This close, she could see the damp glimmer of his eyes on her—eyes that always seemed to open a little too wide. Once, he asked her if she wanted to take a drive with him. It was before the girls, and they'd never gone anywhere together before, but they both got into his pickup truck and drove to Big Bear Mountain—circling the lake once, and then driving home. The air had been fresh, clean, and they'd driven with the windows down so that her hair whipped around her face.

Now they sat in comfortable silence. She knew his fidgety movements, his smells, the timbre of his voice when he cleared his throat, just as he probably knew her movements and sounds and smells. They were two bodies that had met for a time and knew one another completely.

She turned on the heater and it sputtered to life, exhaling a low, hot current through the vents that Packy held his hands up to.

Evelyn opened the glove box and grabbed a granola bar from the pack she kept in the car for Lila. She held it out to Packy, and he looked at her.

"I came back because I made a wrong turn," he said, ignoring the bar.

Evelyn stared, confused.

"That don't make sense," she said.

"I mean you know how sometimes you get driving and you start to think that maybe you went the wrong way, and every mile you drive you're getting farther and farther away from where you're supposed to be?" he said. "I keep feeling like I'm going the wrong way—that you were the good way. You were right. I shouldn't've expected you to just pack up and leave after you'd spent a year taking care of those girls."

Evelyn put the granola bar back in the glove box and shut it with a sharp *snap*. "All of that's passed. No point in going over it again. You left and I stayed."

"I know, I know, I just—" He cut himself off, shoved his flappy hands in his hoodie pocket. He frowned down at his knees in thought, then leaned forward to look through the windshield, up at the yawning black sky. "I'm talking about the double-headed arrow of time. I'm talking about—as we age, our cells replicate over and over again, infinitely, but in the process, they skip over bits and pieces of our DNA. Typos. Those typos build over time and cause disorder, messiness, entropy, and that's what leads to our breakdown. Our pieces slowly falling apart."

Evelyn thought about the morning she woke up to find Packy gone, how she thought he might have just disappeared for a while like he often did, how it took her weeks to realize that he was gone and not coming back. How he left her to figure out his leaving on her own.

"That's what the universe is doing," Packy said. "It's been expanding for fourteen billion years, and that inevitable falling apart—that's the forward-pointing arrow of time. But all of that movement and disorder is moving outward from something, right? The Big Bang. The ultimate compaction—all of the heat and light and matter in the universe condensed into one microscopic particle—and then *bam!* The champagne glass smashing on the floor."

Outside, Evelyn could see Bobby parking his 2002 blue Civic on the other side of the parking lot, half an hour late for his shift. He got out of his car and looked at Evelyn, lifting his hands in a questioning way. Evelyn looked away.

"What if the Big Bang is a place—a membrane? And on the other side of it, time is going in reverse, condensing to that microscopic particle—the backward-pointing arrow of time. The pieces of the broken glass fitting themselves back together. Somewhere on that other side, you and I are both going back to Riverside. Meeting each other at the house. Growing backward, becoming the people we were before. Don't you ever think that? That there are people we're supposed to be with at the same time and place—the same point on the graph?"

Bobby took a few steps toward her car and held his arms out in a more dramatic questioning way. He pointed at the No Loitering sign on the wall.

Evelyn squeezed Packy's arm with a smile. She'd missed his rants and ramblings. Sometimes they were beautiful. "I gotta go."

"Erin OD'd," said Packy.

Evelyn looked at him. He was backlit against the gas pump fluorescents, the side of his face outlined in white so that she could see his grainy three- or four-day growth of beard.

"I called Doris to see about moving back. I asked about Erin and she said Erin is dead."

Evelyn strained to see his face through the darkness. Was he lying to her?

"Come with me. Go get the girls and we'll all leave together," he said.

"To go where?"

"Anywhere. Butte. Seattle. Denver. It doesn't matter."

"Let's talk about it later. I need to get home."

"Let's go now," said Packy, touching her hand. She could feel the faint trembling in his fingers and she knew him well enough to know that there was no reason why he had to leave now. He just got the midnight flight impulse, and if she didn't go with him now, he would go alone.

Evelyn could see them driving away together, the girls in the back seat, driving into the winter sun as it rose hot and white over the eastern mountains, lighting their baby-hair flyaways ablaze. But she said, "I can't."

The trembling in Packy's hand stilled.

"I can't leave Nan," Evelyn said. "I can't leave this place."

Packy was silent. They were both silent.

"Okay," he said. "Then we'll stay." He looked at her. "We'll stay."

Evelyn looked at him, thought of how he'd left without saying goodbye. She said, "I need to think. Where are you staying?"

In the darkness, she could see the phosphene glitter in Packy's eyes as he smiled. "I'll be here when you come back tonight."

And he got out of the car.

NAN

Clara was gone.

The morning light slanted through the stained glass windows as they sat in the church. Nan and Evelyn had taken the girls to Mass, and Jube had come with them, sitting up straight and smiling ahead confidently during the homily as Father LaHargue said that God was like a mother: just as a mother worries about her children and knows where they are at all times, God worries about us, follows us.

When it came time for the parishioners to line up for the Eucharist, Evelyn stayed seated because she hadn't gone to confession—because she wouldn't confess.

Jube walked right to the front of the church and opened her mouth, even though Nan didn't think Jube had ever gone to confession in her life.

Nan had searched for Clara so they could both roll their eyes together, but Clara was nowhere. Nan scanned the pews, the church, but couldn't find Clara.

When they got home, Jube made toast for Lila and Mora and sang "Jingle Bell Rock." She smiled and waggled her eyebrows at

Nan because she knew how much the song annoyed her—how much it annoyed her when people sang Christmas songs after Christmas. Nan grumbled, but Clara wasn't there to chime in with something dry and cutting.

Evelyn was quiet. She'd come home from Mass with a look of restlessness Nan knew. Something in her face had changed, glass cracked beneath a film of tape. She was carrying some terrible weight in her bones and she smiled a wavering smile when Mora tromped across the room to her, arms up.

Lila was feeling better, eyes brighter but still a yellowy, sodium vapor cast to her skin as she sat at the table and ate her toast and asked, "What I'm gonna get next Christmas, Mama?"

Evelyn answered only with a crooked smile, eyes flickering to the windows, to the door, looking for an escape, and that was how Nan knew she was going to leave.

Nan wouldn't ask her when or why.

She went through the day like any other, making snacks for the girls, wiping the crumbs they left behind, playing the piano, and making dinner, all the while watching Evelyn—watching the flighty shift in her eyes, the tensile grip in her shoulders.

As Nan got ready for bed, she tried to tamp down her rising panic.

An empty house again. No Evelyn, no Lila or Mora. Probably no Jube, because why would she stay?

And no Clara. No Peter.

Nan couldn't bear it.

She got out of bed and put on her robe and her slippers. Evelyn didn't have work that night, but Nan knew she wasn't asleep yet, and she padded creakily down the hall to Evelyn's room to tell her that she couldn't bear it if they left. The door was open a few inches and she raised a hand to push it open, but heard the shush of the front door opening and shutting. She froze—she fumbled down the hall. Nothing. No one.

But there: a shadow in the yard.

She went to the window and pulled back the lace curtains. She could see her there in the moonless dark, the steely gleam of her hair, her hunched back as she glided down the rutted road and out of sight. Clara. They hadn't spoken in over a week—not since the night at the lake, and her absence felt like a nerve exposed to cold air.

Nan opened the door and hurried outside, into the night, even though she was wearing only slippers and her ratty, thin zip-up robe.

"Clara," she whispered in the darkness as she hobbled across the frozen grass, hips aching. "Wait!"

By the time she reached the road, Clara was gone. She strained to see through the darkness. Every movement—every shadow-shift, night animals springing in the ferns and brush—caught her eye. But then she spotted Clara at the bottom of the hill, rounding a corner, pretending not to see or hear her.

"Clara," Nan rasped as she jogged after her. "Clara, for God's sake!"

She had to swing her elbows to take the pressure off her hips as she shuffled down the road, icy gravel sliding out from under her feet so that she slipped and skidded through the ruts. She might have fallen—she couldn't tell. She rounded the corner that Clara had taken, hopping on one foot when she took the turn too sharply. She was dizzy, head swinging, and when she steadied herself, she spotted Clara disappearing around another corner up ahead.

If the future was an empty house and no Clara, or an empty house and endless nights of chasing Clara through the streets, always just out of reach, Nan would take the latter, and she hurried after her, lungs aching.

When she got to the bottom of the hill, she dropped her arms and looked around for Clara. She didn't recognize any of the houses around her. She felt a small, warm hand take hers and she looked down to find Peter standing beside her, face tilted up as if looking at her—the way he used to see her without seeing. Something concussed in her chest, the ache of missing. She felt air trying to squeeze through her tight throat. She'd forgotten how small he was.

When he started to pull her, she went with him, letting herself drift along, amazed to once again feel the mathematical precision of the bones of his sweet little hand, to see the back of his neck and the way the hair swept up in a cowlick, like he'd woken from a nap, hair disheveled and flattened, standing up above his right ear. He was pulling her and she was following, no longer feeling her torn feet or the freezing wet of the ground.

He pulled her down hills, up hills, through thick huddles of firs so that her robe and nightgown became soaked and torn. He was taking her to the lake. They walked around yellow larches, stepped over fallen maple trunks and the fungal helixes that had colonized them, ducked under jutting spruce branches. Something gouged her face and she felt blood and stinging open skin.

And then a light came on. Peter was gone—she couldn't feel his hand anymore. She stopped and looked around. She wasn't at the lake; she was in a clearing. She was at a house. She was in a yard. There were lights flashing in the street, blue and red lighting up the night. Someone was coming toward her—a man. He was saying something but her blood was thick and loud in her ears.

"Ma'am," he was saying. "Ma'am."

He was taking her by the elbow and guiding her away. She looked back at the house—whose house? She saw the open front door. Saw Myrna standing on the doorstep, her arms crossed, Terry frowning in disapproval behind her.

EVELYN

Hanging in a half sleep, Evelyn woke when she saw the lights flashing on the trees. She left the girls in bed and went out, hurrying down the hall just as Jube was coming out of her room—T-shirt, no bra. Evelyn opened the front door to find a police officer walking Nan up the frozen grass. She was looking around the house in a dislocated daze, face bleeding, hair snagged with twigs and pine needles. Her robe was soaked and spattered in mud, and as the officer helped her up the porch steps, Evelyn could see that her slippers were shredded and flapping like banana peels.

"She was found wandering in a neighbor's yard," the officer said.

He was saying something else but Evelyn didn't hear anything more as she took Nan inside and sat her down on the couch. Jube must have been the one to shut the front door.

"Nan," Evelyn said, picking leaves out of her hair.

The gash on Nan's cheek was deep and a curtain of blood was slipping down her face and neck. The old fingernail scratches on her neck were now inflamed slices. In another moment, Jube was beside Evelyn holding out a warm wet washcloth that steamed in the dim kitchen light. Evelyn wiped the blood and said, "Nan. Nan."

"He was right there," Nan was saying. "I felt his hand—you know how you can feel their little bones? I felt his bones."

Every time Evelyn swiped at the wound on Nan's cheek, blood beaded up and spilled out again in flashing threads. Evelyn looked at Jube and heard herself croak, "Stitches?" She couldn't get air.

"Nah, just a little tape. Stay there," said Jube, who disappeared and came back minutes later with a piece of duct tape cut into a butterfly bandage. She knelt in front of Nan and taped the wound shut.

Evelyn stood up but Nan grabbed both of her hands.

"I'm not crazy, Evelyn," she said hotly, pupils contracted to pinpricks. She wasn't lost anymore. "I saw him. It was Peter."

She was looking into Evelyn's face, demanding something of her.

"When you go, I won't have anyone. He knows that. Clara knows that," Nan said, squeezing Evelyn's hands.

Evelyn shook her head. "I'm not leaving."

"All right, all right," said Jube, putting both hands on one knee to hoist herself up. "It's late. Let's all go back to bed and talk about it in the morning."

Jube and Evelyn walked Nan to her bedroom and helped her change into a dry nightgown. Evelyn took her torn slippers and Nan snapped, "Don't you even think of throwing those away. I can fix them."

"I wasn't gonna throw em away," Evelyn said.

After she tucked the covers around Nan, she carried the soiled slippers out to the kitchen, wrapped them in a paper towel, and shoved them deep into the trash can.

A social worker was at the front door the next morning. A narrow-nosed man with thin, yellow-orange hair. He said his name was Tom Parker.

Evelyn stood in the doorway, biting her lips as the man said, "I'm here because your neighbor reported an elderly woman wandering into her backyard last night."

"What? Being old is illegal now?" Jube snapped from somewhere behind Evelyn.

"I'm only here because we received a report that she's the primary caregiver of two young children and she's been frequently seen wandering the town. We're legally required to investigate any report. May I come inside?"

Evelyn moved aside and let him in. Mora and Lila were on the couch, watching cartoons, and the man asked, "They're . . . your kids?" He pointed his pen from Evelyn to Jube and back.

"Mine. Yes," said Evelyn.

He scribbled something down on his clipboard. "So who watches them during the day?"

"I do," said Jube, hands on her hips. "Hope that ain't a crime."

The man was writing something, and he looked at Jube over the rim of his glasses but didn't respond. He looked around the house.

"Well, it seems like everything is in order here—but this is the second time we've gotten a report about your childcare situation. If you need any assistance, you can go to this website and apply for subsidized daycare," he said, handing her a card.

She took the card, and out of the corner of her eye, she saw Jube look at her.

Even after he left and Evelyn had watched his car back out of the gravel driveway, she couldn't release the knot that had caught in her throat like a wad of gristle when he said he'd been to the house before.

If social workers were watching them, it was only a matter of time before they learned the truth about the two little girls and who they really belonged to.

Evelyn wasn't a true mother. She was an impostor—a thief—and when she left that night to go to work and saw the bat impaled on the doornail—when she drove down the icy mud road and saw the tall, thin shadow slinking away into the trees—she knew that alive or dead, Erin wanted her girls back.

Packy's truck was in the gas station parking lot, parked in the farthest space at the edge of the lot, overlooking the gorge below and the sharp evergreen points of the forest beyond. His truck was dark, and when Evelyn approached it, she saw that he was asleep inside. She didn't knock on the window.

She went into the gas station and worked her shift, and when she clocked out just before sunrise, she saw that the truck was still there. He would wait. He would give her time to think.

There was a chance there was a baby unfolding somewhere inside her, tissue amassing like stardust—a tiny, sparking nebula. Jamie's baby—the three of them occupying the same point on the time-space grid like Packy said.

She had to talk to Jamie.

She drove away from the gas station and turned north, driving along the perimeter of the lake, under the dripping trees, under the cormorants perched and watching with their reared heads and sidelong gazes. She steered up into the hills of the north shore, past the old Victorians that were built by the railroad and logging families—the robber barons who seized land and built empires with grim ruthlessness.

She came to Ursula's house and stopped halfway down

the driveway. The curtains of nearly every window were open and people were moving around inside. Smoke was coming from the chimney and she could see the TV flickering in the living room. A man was sitting on the sofa, feet propped up on an ottoman. He looked at her through the front window and she backed out of the driveway quickly. She saw him jump off the couch, but she sped away before he got to the front door.

She drove down the hill toward the lake, not knowing where she was going. Had the family come home early? Had they found Jamie there?

Jamie.

She grabbed her phone, but realized she didn't have his number. She didn't know where he lived. She didn't even know his last name.

He didn't know anything about her either—couldn't contact her if he wanted to.

She pulled onto the side of the road, beneath the reaching blue boughs of the firs and hemlocks that lined the road so thickly that it was impossible to tell one from another. She opened her door and got out of the car to gulp the cold air. The bracing lake wind was sharp with a pine forest smell, and she looked at the clear morning sky—golden, a wind-swept plain.

She got her phone out of the car and called the club. Tanya answered.

"Is Jamie coming in today?" Evelyn asked.

"Was he your child's swim instructor?" Tanya asked. She didn't recognize Evelyn's voice. "His employment at the club ended nearly a month ago."

"Do you have his phone number?" Evelyn asked. "I need to—"

But Tanya had already hung up.

Evelyn stood rooted in place, understanding that Jamie had disappeared into the mist, and as she slumped back inside the car, she felt the wetness in her underwear, the twisting cramps in the bowl of her pelvis, and looked down to see the blood seeping through her jeans.

The pines swayed in the wind as the cold sank into the car, and Evelyn waited, listened.

Nothing. There was nothing there.

The trees lining the road towered two hundred feet high and created a corridor through the mountains, all of it yawning open to a wide, impossibly deep sky. Evelyn started the car and drove, the small, flaring galaxy inside of her collapsing on itself—a black hole. No baby—no possibility of a baby. Just the endless depth of sky, the endless depth inside her.

When she got home, it was snowing—light, floating flakes. As she pulled into the yard, she saw Jube in the backyard holding Lila, who was wrapped up in a bundle of blankets. Lila had probably had another coughing fit and Jube had brought her outside to let the cold air open her lungs.

Jube set the girl on the wooden bench by the flowerbed— Evelyn could only see Lila's white forehead and a tufty wisp of red curls—and went back inside the house.

Something slid out of the jagged aspens—a tall, thin shadow—a woman, long legs, long arms, skeletal in a pair of stained jeans and a saggy tank top. Her brushy, red hair flapped in the snow as Erin took three large, lurching steps toward Lila, reaching for her.

"Erin!" Evelyn yelled, running, and sliding through the snowy grass toward Lila. Erin looked at her, eyes huge and deep and empty—asteroidal craters—mummified cheekbones, lips thin and drawn back from long teeth. She took three large stork-steps backward, dissolving in the trees that stood like lean-ing femurs in the mist, and Evelyn scooped up Lila, whose lips had gone blue. She wasn't breathing.

If Erin couldn't have her alive, she'd have her dead.

Erin was drowning her.

THE LEAVING

Evelyn moved quickly, silently, because she knew now what she needed to do. She stuffed their clothes in a trash bag, grabbed toys and shoes, Barbies and Hot Wheels and jackets, too focused on what she was doing to notice the tilt of the house, the sounds of movement coming from Nan's room—was that a window opening? The front door opening and shutting? Evelyn opened the bedroom door and peered down the hall. Darkness, silence. She grabbed the nebulizer, put the albuterol on ice in a sandwich baggie, and carried everything out to the car, stepping lightly, rocking heel to toe so her footsteps wouldn't wake anyone.

Lila and Mora wouldn't be safe until they got away from Cormorant Lake.

Evelyn carried Mora out first, wrapping her in one of Nan's afghans and buckling her into her car seat. Her head tipped back and her mouth dropped open as she snored. Evelyn went back in for Lila and wrapped her in the bedspread, carrying her out to the car and buckling her in.

She started the car and drove away from the house slowly, gravel crunching underneath, and down the mud road, knowing that Nan would be broken. This would break her. But Evelyn had to get Lila and Mora out of that house. Besides, there was Jube—Jube would help put Nan's pieces back together.

Evelyn would go to the gas station. She would find Packy and they would leave.

As she drove down the road, her headlights lit on the flash of a nightgown disappearing into the trees. Muddy, bare feet. Nan. Followed by a pack of dogs—Rosie and the yapping Chihuahuas. And then someone ran across the road after her. Jube.

Evelyn stopped the car and tried to peer through the shadows after them. She saw pine branches rolling, ferns shivering off chunks of ice. She grabbed the wheel, but couldn't take her foot off the brake—couldn't leave Nan and Jube out in the cold like that.

She got out and left the car idling, doors open, as she grabbed Lila and Mora from the back seat. Carrying them one on each hip, she went into the dripping trees after her mothers.

She would take them with her—Nan and Jube. They could leave together. She could hold them all. Nan would get a fresh start somewhere new—would get away from the death and guilt that had kept her tied to this place all these years. Jube could start over too, and maybe Evelyn could learn to love her.

They were following a road up the hill, and Evelyn tried to keep up, walking quickly in the blue starlight that glanced off the ice and snow, almost running. Did she hear piano music? A quickening tempo? She could hear Nan and Jube ahead of her as their legs crashed through scrub and bracken, and a sound rose up from the woods, from the lake beyond. A seismic rumble. The crushing shift of bedrock. And something that sounded like a voice—a windy moan.

But she couldn't keep up with them, and by the time the sagging Tooley mansion came into view with its blacked-out turret and mossy, caved-in roof, Jube and Nan had disappeared.

Evelyn stood still, holding the two little girls who were awake now and gripping her shirt, shivering, their tiny breaths puffing out in hot clouds along with her own. Evelyn looked around the dark grounds, but there was no sign of Jube or Nan anywhere. And then, from somewhere behind the house: a sigh.

Evelyn followed the sound around the greenhouse to a ledge overlooking the lake, to a rotting, wooden handrail that Jube was gripping as she looked down at the water below—at the inverted night of the black lake, the snowy mountains that soared downward to the starry black sky at the bottom—the backward-moving arrow of time that would take them back to the point of origin.

And Evelyn could see—cutting the surface of the lake—a boat, coasting serenely along the membrane between the two worlds. Nan.

Evelyn looked at the ledge they were standing on—no bridge, no steps. It was a straight, two-hundred-foot drop.

"How'd she get down there?" she asked Jube.

"I thought it was her." Jube was trembling. "I thought it was her I was following."

A sound rose from the lake. A loud thunder crack from deep within the earth that echoed in lapping waves through the mountains and rolled into a slow, deep pulse. A bass A minor. The lake-bottom heartbeat of the beast that had once shrugged off whole mountainsides of cedars, that had once spewed lava that incinerated the valley and flowed all the way out to the sea—it was down there, and with each shuddering boom of the heartbeat, a light flickered somewhere deep in the black water. A volcanic vent. The electrical circuits of a falling train.

The light flickered and the groaning moaning woman-wail bubbled up from the bottom, and Nan stood up in the boat and called to it, "I'm here." Leaning. "It's me. I'm here!"

ACKNOWLEDGMENTS

I'm so grateful to Writing by Writers for giving me the opportunity to learn from some of the most inspiring writers, as well as for giving me the confidence to keep moving forward on draft seventeen or eighteen of this book.

Endless thanks to Lea Gibson, Claire Vath, Daphne Tanouye, and Kate Blythe for reading early drafts of this story and taking the time to give thorough and unflinching feedback.

Thanks to my agent, the Inimitable Pamela Malpas, for seeing exactly what I wanted to do with this book and fighting for that vision—as well as to my editor, Corinna Barsan, for having a perfect mind meld with me in the revision process.

My deepest thanks to the entire Blackstone team for their incredible work.

Thank you, Mickey and John Riley, for providing free childcare so I could go sit in my car in a parking lot somewhere and write.

Thank you, Mom, for buying me endless stacks of paper and the exact pens I preferred.

And to Jack, Edwin, and Travis: thank you for everything.